The Gambling Man

The Gambling Man

R.M. LITCHFIELD

A Black Horse Western

ROBERT HALE · LONDON

ISBN 0 7090 6653 8

Robert Hale Limited
Clerkenwell House
Clerkenwell Green
London EC1R 0HT

Typeset by
Derek Doyle & Associates, Liverpool.
Printed and bound in Great Britain by
WBC Book Manufacturers Limited, Bridgend.

To my brothers and sisters, outlaws and in-laws, Doreen and Jack, Pamela and Jim, Cindy and Bob, and Jessica, with all my love and grateful thanks for 'the happy highways where I went and cannot come again'.

One

There's nothing worse than dying with the knowledge that you have been a fool. It's something you don't really have time to get over, and as Kirk Langley fell backwards, drowning in his own blood, he thought sadly, well, I sure screwed up again. And how. There was almost time, as his glazing eyes registered his last sight on earth – the little Chinese dude padding softly across the floor towards him to retrieve his hardware – to realize that he'd been at his most foolish when he thought he had been most clever. Oh, shit, was his very last thought. Not very original, but it summed up well the position he had gotten himself into. . . .

Kirk had been confident when the Chinaman walked in that he, Kirk Langley, was for the first time in his rather unimpressive career was going to be calling the shots. For years he'd been Clay Brunton's gofer. Time to change things.

The way it was, Kirk was the only guy there at the mine who tumbled to what happened – no one else. And he had hugged that secret to himself all the way back to town, and the warmth of the secret and his gloating self-congratulatory back-slapping had led to carelessness,

7

and carelessness had led to this, and this was a lonely, squalid death, kicking and choking his life away on the floor of a Chinese gambling den.

When the Chinee had walked in Kirk had thought, hell, he ain't even armed, musta stashed his shotgun at the mine or outside in the stable, and he's wearin' ridin' gloves, so if he does have a gun hidden away, he's gonna have to take those off, even 'fore he starts digging in his heathen tunic for it. Boy howdy! I got the drop on him an' I gonna take him for all he's got.

Just the same, Kirk kept his hand close to his Colt, for though Chung Wah was not a big guy, he had presence. Kirk had once been in Deadwood, in a poker game that Hickok had sat in on when a cigar drummer had folded. Hickok had turned those eyes on Kirk after he had scooped a good pot, and Kirk had felt iced water run down his spine. Now, as he told Chung what he had seen at the mine, how he had put it all together, and what he wanted in return for his silence, he saw in those obsidian black eyes the same fierce but controlled anger, though the Chinese gambler's face remained impassive, nor did Chung's voice betray his feelings.

'You have much knowledge, and that can be dangerous,' Chung Wah warned. 'What do you want in exchange for your silence?'

Kirk told him then, and the young Chinese man laughed openly, 'All?' he asked, with a sweep of his arm, taking in the room, the tables prepared, some for an evening's fan-tan, others for dice or dominoes, and, should any friendly Westerners wander in (though they were few and far between since the railway had been built and the Chinese no longer needed), poker, Chung Wah's favourite game. 'Just walk away with the clothes I am wearing? I give you *everything*?'

Kirk grinned, his thin, mean face only looking more pitiless, more stupid.

'Not everything,' he said in what he hoped was a firm voice, trying to sound like his boss, Clay Brunton, well, his ex-boss if this came off. 'You get to keep yer life, if you move fast. They's a last train out tonight.'

Even as he spoke there came the long-drawn-out sound of the train's whistle from across town as it pulled out of the depot – *whoo-wah*, a lonesome sound, Kirk always thought, and he itched to draw his pocket watch from his waistcoat, check what he already knew – the damn watch was slow again. But that would mean taking his hand off the butt of his pistol.

Whoo-wah, went the locomotive as it wound its way round the mountain side, and the Chineseman spread his gloved hands sadly, in a gesture of futility. And from the palm of his right glove flew a little shining silver star. With pointy ends, Kirk noticed. Little pointy ends that shone brightly as it spun oh, so quickly across the room and took him square in the chest, over the heart. Kirk didn't even have time to go for his gun, but scrabbled at his shirt front like he was trying to swat a yellerjacket that had stung him, staring the while at Chung Wah who had shed his gloves and was now effortlessly spinning another of his little shiny stars at Kirk. This one caught him full under the chin, slicing into his throat, and the blood welled up and drowned the man as he fell to the floor, thinking what a fool he'd been.

'You see,' Chung Wah confided as he leant over to retrieve his star-knives, wiping them clean on the dead man's shirt, 'You are not a good gambler. You must be sure of the other man's hand before you stake all. And you would have boasted too, long before I got clear. Now

I . . .' He spun round as the slightest of coughs sounded behind him.

In the doorway leading to his private quarters stood the girl, dressed in a yellow *cham song*. Chung suppressed his usual irritation with her as she stood in the way she had been taught to before men, head bowed, eyes downcast, hands folded before her, awaiting her master's pleasure. Her thoughts, of course, were her own, and she had long ago found it best to keep them that way.

'What is it?' Chung asked. He stepped to one side as he spoke, and the girl saw the dead man for the first time. Her hand flew up to her mouth and she gasped with shock.

'Who he?' she asked.

'A stupid *gweh loh* who thought he was cleverer than a Chinese man,' Chung said. Now what the hell do I do with him, he thought. They're already attacking Chinese on the streets at night. Two had been lynched last week by drunken townsfolk. If this was discovered, not only he, Chung Wah, would dance on a rope. He owed it to his countrymen to find a safe resting place for Kirk Langley.

'You kill?' the girl queried.

'Yes, I killed him,' Chung Wah snapped, stressing his correct English. The girl had been told to speak the *gweh loh* language at all times, but she often lapsed into her native Cantonese dialect. Chung had impressed on her the need to learn English. The hard way. Now she never forgot, though it was somewhat basic still.

'What you do?'

'I don't godamn know!' Chung shouted. There was no need to keep his composure in front of a lowly slave-girl.

'Soon gamblers come,' the girl said.

The realization that his gambling palace, the Gam Saan, would soon be thronged with Chinese labourers from the mines, eager to risk their meagre wages at the tables, spurred Chung to think quickly.

He wanted the place, Chung Wah thought, looking down at the dead body of Kirk Langley. Well, he can have it.

'Quick,' he hissed at the girl, 'bring bucket, water, cloths. Clean up the blood, bring a shovel from the stable. We'll bury him right here.' And he began pulling up the floorboards close to the corpse.

'Shovel?' the girl repeated. 'What is shovel?'

'Stupid dog!' Chung shouted. 'You know nothing? A shovel is the thing you clean out horse shit from the stable with. Now get it – quick, or you'll feel my hand!'

The girl bowed meekly. 'Yes, master,' she said. Stupid, sawn-off little prick, she thought. In her own language, of course.

At the door she turned. 'Wei Yip come while you at mine,' she told him. 'He say tell you leper nun come on noon train.'

Despite all his problems Chung Wah smiled to himself as he prepared what he hoped was Kirk Langley's final resting place.

'Now *that* is good news,' the gambler whispered in the dead man's ear as he dragged him sideways to see if the hole in the boards was big enough. Kirk was too busy being dead to answer.

TWO

Not everyone regarded the leper nun as good news, however. When she stumped down the platform at 'Frisco railroad depot to catch her train, folks scattered like chaff in a hurricane. No wonder, really. She was something, the leper nun, really something. A short dame, with a yellow habit and a huge crucifix round her neck, a white apron, and that thick veil that made her look like some crazy ghost. She limped along with the aid of a knotty wooden staff taller than herself, from which hung a small bell that announced her presence, should anyone be blind, or stupid enough, not to have seen her coming a mile away. With her she had an old, crippled Chinese guy who limped before her, waving a collecting box and a crudely-lettered sign that read: 'This famous Mother Chu, the leper nun. Please give for heathen lepers'. One look at the old man, who made much play on the stumps where several of his fingers should have been and a number of deathly white blotches on his face, neck and arms, then a quick look at the weird nun, and the gawkers on the platform gave her room, although no donations were forthcoming.

'Lookit her now,' one waster observed from a safe lounging point. 'Why's she walk s'durned gimpy?'

'Had her feet bound, like all them Chinee broads,' his friend speculated.

'Nah, she got the leprosy too,' the waster replied.

'How kin you tell?'

'Cain't rightly,' the waster confessed. 'But she's wearin' gloves too, in this heat. Guess she lost a few fingers, well as toes out there. Wanna bet I'm right?'

Almost as if she had sensed their speculation the leper nun paused and turned her veiled head in the direction of the two idlers. Beneath the veil could be seen indistinctly the dull sheen of black goggles. The two loafers suddenly remembered something urgent they had to do someplace else and left the platform to the leper nun and her crippled attendant.

And that was the reception the weird pair got all the way along the platform and on to the train, and although on certain stages along the way the rest of the train was packed, no one chose, after a hasty glance into her compartment, to travel with the leper nun. Didn't put anything in the collecting box neither.

But the strange couple did arrive rested and refreshed, and to some reception, for the telegraphists along the line had passed the word with their incessant, nervous, tapping gossip and when the pair alighted from the train in the high mountain mining town they were gawked at by half the population of that place – from a safe distance. No one stepped forward to check their tickets, no one offered to help an old lady and a cripple with their baggage. There was no one to meet and welcome them.

The bell on her staff tinkling, the leper nun hobbled painfully down the platform clutching her own carpet-bag and in the company of her attendant she walked down dusty Main Street to Jackson Row and off into the

Chinese quarter, where, given the present tension between the Chinese and the townsfolk, none chose to follow.

That week's *Weekly Thunderer* thundered, none too weakly, in its *Town Talk* column:

Those least desired immigrants ever to wash up on our fine country's shore, namely the Chinese, filthy, disagreeable and undesirable in all ways, have long infested our town. To be sure there was a use for them when we needed a railroad to be brought here, but Soe-Sli and his tribe, having built that railroad and having been well paid for it, have outstayed their welcome. They work in the mines for less pay and longer shifts than white miners. If they work their own mines they thrive where a white man starves, and when they have destroyed mining for the white man, why they move into commerce, gambling, restaurants.

Whose town is this, ours or Johnny Chinee's? They are an encumbrance that we well know how to rid ourselves of, and events over the last few weeks show that some public-spirited men of this town know how to effect this best, for every time a 'hemp committee' has invited another Chinee to attend a 'necktie party', more of the yellow devils leave town on the morrow's train. Now we hear that the notorious gambler, miner and labour organizer, Chung Wah (what names they have!), has advised his fellow countrymen, those not bound by contract to the larger mines in the area, to return to San Francisco, whose townsfolk are welcome to them. We further understand that Mr Wah has been liquidating his own interests in the area, and has

recently sold his gold mine to that sporting gentle-
man and saloon owner, Mr Brunton.

The Chinese nun who caused such a sensation
when she arrived in town yesterday has not surfaced
at any of our places of worship yet, but stays
immured in Chinatown. We feel entitled to ask the
following questions of our mayor and council:
What is the nun doing here? Ministering to lepers
in the very heart of our community? Just how
infected is our unwelcome Chinese population?
What are our appointed officials doing to ensure
that the disease will not strike amongst the white
folk of this town, and just when will these unclean
heathens be told to 'git', *en masse?*

The editor, a thwarted politician, would have been the
first to admit that, apart from the lynching in town of two
Chinese mineworkers, it had been a quiet week, and the
nun helped fill a column and a half of town gossip where
there was none. Plus, it got at the mayor and council,
whom the editor cordially detested. Sometimes he
wondered who he hated most – them or the Chinese.

Three

Johnny Beamis, on the other hand, quite liked the Chinese. No, correction, he loved them like brothers. Ever since the affair a year ago, up at the Golconda Mine. Johnny had been new in the area, drifted in prospecting for gold. He'd trekked over that day from his claim on Robb Creek to buy some dynamite and caps from the mine superintendent at the Golconda and to have their assayer run tests on what he thought was some promising ore he'd blown out with the last of his explosives – turned out to be worthless, running at less than a dollar a ton – and was on his way back down the narrow trail when something spooked his mule, old Number Nine.

Could have been the coolies standing by an air vent, could have been a snake, but whatever, Number Nine tore the lead-rein from Johnny's hand and took off down a steep slope of over two hundred feet, the incline about one in three, over shale and loose rocks that would have fazed anything less ornery than a mule. Braying and bawling, the packs bouncing up and down, the mule set off at a fair lick, then began digging its heels in to slow its momentum, whilst hop-jumping over the boulders that lay in its way down to the next level piece of ground. All in all, it was quite spectacular.

16

Johnny should have been concerned, but he wasn't. The moment old Number Nine took off a gleam came into his eye, and he leaned forward, licked his lips and watched so intently that he was blind to all else around him.

You see, Johnny was a born gambler. What he was doing was computing the odds on the mule making the bottom still upright.

He'd been that way since he could remember. One of his earliest memories had been betting his older sister that the black beetle he'd caught in the stable could outrun any other she put up. It did, too, and he won a stick of candy, while Sis squashed both bugs and cried. Sore loser. That didn't deter Johnny, and while other kids learnt their math in the old log schoolhouse back home and played 'cracking the whip' or tiggie at playtime, Johnny learnt to compute odds from an unsuspecting teacher during lessons and perfected his shuffle and deal with a dog-eared pack of cards behind the boy's outhouse during recess.

It wasn't that he was greedy for money, or too lazy to work for it. It was just that when Johnny was gambling his heart beat a little faster and the day seemed brighter. Life was worth living when the odds put an edge on it, he found. If there was no one else to bet against he'd bet against himself. A born gambler.

So, leaning over the edge of the mountain track and watching a goodly proportion of his entire worldly possessions disappearing at a fair rate downhill, Johnny silently computed the odds, and with absolute absorption in the scene before him muttered quietly to himself, 'Five dollars evens says he makes it to the bottom without falling over and breaking his fool neck.'

'Bet taken,' came a voice behind him, and an ivory-

coloured, calloused hand was proffered and shaken
absent-mindedly by Johnny, who, concerned that the
mule seemed to be losing some of the elasticity in its
hind legs, was now watching its rapid descent of the
mountain-side with even more interest. Five dollars now
rode on Number Nine's back.

'And me fi' dollar,' came another voice, another proffered paw to shake. Johnny shook. The game was getting
interesting.

'An' me . . . an' me . . . an' me. . . .' Pretty soon every
man jack amongst the Chinese work-crew who had been
enjoying a quiet smoke in the airshaft was jostling
Johnny either to take his bet or was leaning over the
edge shouting ribald comments on the mule's poor
chance of negotiating the descent. Johnny was transfixed; he stood to win close on a hundred dollars if his
mule could just hang in there, and for the first time in
their short relationship, Johnny felt something akin to
affection for the brute. At the same time Johnny felt a
warmth towards the company he had fallen in with. It
was like coming home at last, meeting so many other
natural gamblers, and he would have agreed, once he
got to know a few more of the Chinese, with the head of
San Francisco Police's Chinatown Police Department,
who said in frustration to a newsman once, 'As long as
there is a Chinaman alive there will be gambling. It is
just as easy to stop a duck from swimming as a Chinese
from gambling.'

Drybread.

Onward and downward, determined as only a mule
can be, plunged the steadfast Number Nine. The miners'
cheering dwindled as the mule neared the bottom, and
Johnny's exhortations could now be heard. Pretty soon,
with only about twenty feet to go, his was the only voice,

and the Chinese had faces longer than pumped water.

'Hang in there, Number Nine!' Beamis urged, 'Only twenty feet to go, buddy!'

Now, mules have damned good hearing, and are anything but slow when it comes to savvying out a situation. Whether Number Nine understood what was happening and decided to play the gamblers up is open to argument, but as it reached the path at the base of the slope it did a strange thing.

It stopped. Stopped dead, with the dust of its descent settling around it, and stood, stock still, with its fore legs on the flat and its hind legs still resting on the mountain side. And then an even stranger event occurred, which would be argued over for some while.

The mule simply vanished. One moment it was there, craning its neck forward to bellow, in triumph or relief or defiance, or maybe even to chew on some greenery, the next moment, with a blinding flash of light and a solid *whumph!*, it disappeared, with nothing remaining, apart from a rather large hole in the ground and a wafting cloud of white smoke, to show where it had once stood.

There is, when carrying explosives and detonators together, danger of a thing called 'sympathetic detonation', that is, the detonators go up, and the explosives follow. Experienced miners and prospectors – which Johnny was not – try, on the whole, to avoid sympathetic detonations. That is what had happened in the close vicinity of old Number Nine. One pack on the back of the mule had exploded and the other had gone up in sympathy. In sympathy with the first pack, of course. Not with the mule.

Painless, but rather undignified, as a way to shuffle off this mortal coil.

There was little sympathy for the mule higher up the

slope, either. Johnny maintained that Number Nine had finished the course and so he should win the wagered money. The Chinese work-crew held that as the mule still had its back legs on the mountainside they should be paid. 'Mule not finish – we win,' their spokesman insisted, holding out his hand for payment.

Johnny didn't like to tell them that the mule was his only collateral and besides that he had only a few cents left in the world. The Chinese forbore to inform Johnny before the bet was laid that, should the wager go against them, they would be similarly embarrassed. They sent most of their money home to China to support their families, what was left after paying that shark Chung Wah.

And so the argument raged on, fierce but slow, as only one man amongst the Chinese could speak English, and that guy acted as interpreter to put each Chinese miner's view on the matter, and each one had a different way of arguing that they had won.

'Look,' Johnny finally said, 'if they was a finishing tape down there for the mule to break, then he would have broke it. End of story. I won. Pay me.'

The translator translated. The Chinese fulminated. The translator drew breath to continue, when . . .

'Excuse me, sir, but can I be of any assistance?'

Johnny turned to see who had spoken. There was no one there. Then he looked down, from his lofty height of six foot three, to see, coming just above his middle waistcoat button, a Chinese guy, smiling like hell and proffering his hand. Johnny took it.

'Chung Wah at your service,' the man informed him, and Johnny introduced himself. When the new arrival had been apprised of the situation, he turned to talk to his fellow countrymen. They seem to have a lot of respect for the little feller, Johnny thought. Maybe he can get my money. Though he doubted it, the way those guys had been talking. Might even come to a fight, they were all so het up.

'These men say it is OK for me to be the judge as to who won the wager,' Chung Wah said to Johnny. 'Will you accept my decision too?'

They stood and weighed each other up. The Chinese man looked at Beamis, six-three in his stockinged feet, lanky and rawboned with a shock of bright red hair and green eyes, his long nose peeling from the sun. A true *gweh loh*, Chung Wah thought. Yet he loves to gamble. And he warmed to the man.

Johnny saw a youngish guy, short even among the Chinese who worked some of the mines around the mountain. Yet he was stocky and stood confidently, and his ebony-black eyes were unwavering.

Johnny stroked his jaw slowly. 'Waal,' he said after a moment's deliberation. 'I sure don't want to offend you, friend, but I don't know you from Adam, and, if you'll excuse a personal observation. . . ?'

'Sure,' Chung Wah said. 'Be as personal as you like.' His eyes, however, told Johnny that maybe it wouldn't be a very good idea to offend the little dude.

'Well, I'd have to be blind not to notice you're Chinese,' Johnny said.

'And? Your point is?'

Johnny looked a mite embarrassed. 'Waal,' he drawled, turning to wave his hand towards the waiting work-crew. 'These guys are Chinese too.'

'I'm going to have grant you that,' Chung Wah acknowledged with a smile. 'Yes, they are all Chinese, though, wait a moment. . . someone may have sneaked a Japanese in there while I wasn't looking. No, all Chinese. You are right.'

'Don't that, make you kind of ... biased? In their favour?' Johnny asked.

'Let me introduce myself – Chung Wah – I am the labour agent hereabouts,' Chung Wah said, bowing to Beamis. 'I am the contractor who brings these men over. I represent my uncle, who is the man who arranges everything in China. Here, I see everything goes OK with the men's employers, translate, and so on. I see everything is fair for both sides.' He forbore to tell Johnny that out of this indentured labour, tantamount to slavery, Chung Wah and his uncle were growing very rich, while their countrymen worked for low wages in dangerous and arduous labour.

'So,' Chung Wah said, 'I have, as you say in America, a foot in both camps. I shall decide fairly, I promise, Mr. . . ?'

'Beamis, Johnny Beamis,' Johnny said, and without thinking stuck out his hand. Chung Wah blinked, then took the proffered paw. In all his dealings with the white man this was the first who had ever offered his hand in a spirit of equality. Even when he had been dealing with the railroad bosses or the mine owners and cooking up deals that made the white fellers rich and successful, they had not deigned to offer their hands. They had looked down on him, and even as he had bowed and made polite noises Chung Wah's spirit had burned within him. He knew what a handshake meant to a Westerner, what insult they offered him by not affording him that simple dignity.

There was a reason why Johnny offered his hand. The reason was: he didn't give a shit. If a guy was OK, then Johnny was OK with him, and if he was black or blue or had his ass tied in a bow it didn't matter to Johnny. What really mattered was: did the guy want to play a game of chance for money? He had a feeling now, as he took the little Chinese guy's hand that here was a man who liked taking risks.

'So,' Chung Wah asked, 'will you accept my judgement? If you don't, then we are both in trouble, Mr Beamis, for they will not pay you, and I will be in big trouble with the mine owners for allowing these men to be idle so long.'

'OK,' Johnny agreed. 'I'll bide by your word.'

Chung Wah bowed his head politely, turned to one side and briefly conferred with the work-crew, then turned back to Johnny. 'Mr Beamis?'

'Johnny.'

'Then, Johnny, your story, please. What was the bet, exactly? Please try to remember your words. You see, in gambling a man's word is like a contract in business. We must see what you both contracted to pay out on.'

Hell, thought Johnny. This was one cute little feller. Not much got past him, he'd bet.

'Let's see,' he mused, stroking his chin. 'I said, near as I 'member, "Five dollars evens the mule makes it to the bottom without falling over and breaking its neck".'

'I see,' Chung Wah said, 'and they took it on that understanding?'

'Hell,' Johnny snapped, 'they were like to snatch m'damned hand off!'

Chung Wah chuckled softly and then turned to the crew. They parleyed a while in their lingo then Chung turned away from them all and stood for a minute or two, thinking to himself. He's a posey bastard, thought Beamis; he's made his mind up already, just doing this to build himself up.

Eventually Chung came back to them and looked gravely at all assembled. 'It is not easy to do fair by both sides,' he said. 'I must clear something up with my countrymen.'

He talked at length, and when he spoke again to Johnny it was evident from the long faces behind him that Chung's decision did not match their hopes. 'I have decided that the mule *did* reach the bottom, as agreed in the bet.'

'*All right!*' Johnny smiled, but the little guy held his hand up to stop him.

'However,' he said firmly, 'the mule did not have both feet off the slope, so it could be said to have only half-completed the course. So, I have decided that the men should only pay you *half* their stakes.'

'What? You mean. . . ?'

Chung nodded. 'It is fair, and, between ourselves, you won't get a red cent any other way.'

'But . . .' Johnny ran a bony hand through his mop of red hair.

'There is another little problem,' Chung said gravely.

'Oh, yeah,' Johnny snapped. 'What's that? You want the mule to run it again?'

'That would be rather difficult,' the little man said gravely. 'No. the problem is that the men don't have any money to pay you with.'

'You're snowing me!' Johnny nigh on yelled.

'Snowing?' For all his command of the American vernacular, Chung Wah was lost.

'Yeah – bullshitting.'

'Ah, yes. . . . This bullshit I know,' Chung Wah said. 'I do have a solution, if you would like to hear it?'

'You bet,' Johnny said grimly.

'Tomorrow night is pay-night,' Chung said. 'You come to my gambling house, the Gam Saan, off Jackson, in the Chinese Quarter, and these men will be there and pay you.'

'Gam Saan?'

'Yeah. In Chinese it means "Golden Mountain". Good name, huh? You will come?'

'Well . . .' Johnny began doubtfully, 'I. . . .'

'You like to play poker?' Chung Wah was a good judge of men. He noted the light come on in Beamis's eyes and smiled. 'Me too,' Chung Wah said. 'So do others – Americans invented the game, but they can't play as good as Chinese.'

'We'll see tomorrow night,' Johnny grinned, sticking his hand out again. 'Now I got to go find me a replacement mule and get some more explosive. Damn shame about that critter, even if he did kick an' bite like the devil. He was a pure-bred mule, all the way from ol' Mexico, where they breed the best.'

Chung Wah turned southward and squinted up into the sky. 'Should be just about back there by now,' he said.

Four

A year or so later Johnny was still going down to Chung Wah's and he was still trying to get his money off the work-crew. Tonight as he stepped inside he saw three of the guys, Loo Wen, So Mah and Dho Lee, who were playing a ferocious, fast game of dominoes for small stakes. They waved him over, but he waved back and made for the far tables, where a number of different card games was in progress. There was no way he was going to put his poke of gold dust down in a dominoes game with those three. They'd have the shirt off his back in an hour or less, just as they'd done that first night. It beat him, how guys with minds like razors, gamblers who could tell what was in your hand and bet accordingly, were bonded workers, slogging their guts out every day God sent, first on the backbreaking work of building a railroad, now in the blistering depths of the Golconda mine.

'Our families have to eat,' So Mah had said, simply.

'My parents are old, cannot work,' Dho Lee had added. And that was it.

'Thy face is as a baboon's arse, red-haired foreign devil,' a hugely fat Chinese man whose face was cratered with smallpox scars said to Johnny in Cantonese.

'Thy mother should marry thy father, were it not

26

incest,' Johnny replied in halting Cantonese. 'Eat your rice and your poxy face will clear up.'

The fat man bellowed with laughter. 'Who taught you that one, *gweh loh*?' he asked.

'Chung Wah,' Johnny replied. 'After I taught him how to play poker!'

'Not bad,' the fat man replied. He nodded towards a distant table. 'We play fan-tan later, maybe? I take you for everything you got.'

'Got to take those guys' money first,' Beamis replied, waving a hand towards the back of the room, where Chung Wah was sitting with a couple of other Chinese.

Chung Wah was ready. Despite his nervousness over the sale of the mine and the killing of Kirk Langley, he was supremely confident that this, his last night in town, was going to be one to remember. Upstairs in his shrine room he had burnt inscriptions written on paper before his guardian spirits. The papers beseeched the spirits to bring his ventures success, and had been written on white paper instead of the usual lucky red. White is the colour of mourning in China, and Chung Wah, like other owners of Chinese gaming-houses, used white throughout to jinx the opposition. Later he had prayed long and hard to the beautiful statue of Kuan Yin his uncle had sent him from Kwangchow. She was his favourite joss or idol, and when the smoke from the incense he had lit changed course and began to drift from Kuan Yin to another of his favourite idols, Kuan Ti, the god of war and a god most honoured by the criminal gangs of Canton, then Chung Wah knew he would have a good night, that everything would go according to plan. Even so, when he came out to eat he had the girl serve him in silence, and he did not reach out for anything until she left the room, for fear she would touch his hand inadvertently and break his luck.

Oh, yes, he thought, as he smiled at Johnny, making his way through the crowd, he might be leaving, but he intended to go out having beaten everyone, the white men with their mines and their hatred of the Chinese, and the gamblers who crowded the Gam Saan every weekend trying to take his money from him, trying to make he, Chung Wah, less than them. Didn't they know who they dealt with? Well, after these last few days' work, rounded off by tonight's gambling, all would remember and talk about him. For a moment he felt fear when he thought what might happen to him if the plan went wrong, if his enemies caught up with him; then he thought, courage, little man, you still have the leper nun as your ace in the hole. And he smiled again, rose to welcome Johnny to the table.

'Johnny, good evening,' Chung Wah greeted him. The other two men at the table followed suit, Quang Ho the restaurateur, and Ki Shing, a hard-bitten-looking little guy who ran a grocery and hardware store in the Quarter, and a small brothel in the back for Chinese only, and who rarely spoke to Johnny even after all this time playing poker together. He seemed to hate Beamis for being white, loved to take his money when Johnny lost to him. Johnny for his part respected the man for being a damn fine poker player, and mentally shrugged when he felt Ki Shing's eyes burn through him. His problem, Johnny thought as he sat down to play.

'Evening, Wah,' Johnny greeted Chung Wah. Time was he'd called the man by his first name, till Chung Wah had told him Chinese folk had their last names first and their first names last. Confusing.

Chung Wah waved his hand in the air and a barman appeared with a tray, four glasses and Johnny's favourite tipple, old Chinese peach brandy, warming and fragrant. Close to heaven as you can get, he thought, sipping it now.

'Straight draw poker, no limit, gentlemen?' Wah asked, breaking the seal on a new deck of cards. No one bothered to answer. It was all they ever played.

Johnny sat back in his chair, put a hand into his vest pocket and threw down his bag of gold dust on to the table in front of him. Three pairs of eyes followed the poke down, gauging its value.

'Winning it ain't gonna be easy, fellers,' Johnny teased. 'I had to work damned hard for it, and so should you!'

'Feel lucky tonight, huh?' Quang Ho grunted as he drew his cards towards him.

Johnny frowned. He never spoke of luck when he was playing. To boast that way was foolish, for it could put an opponent on his mettle, make him more alert and determined to win. Or, if he was the touchy type and losing badly it could be seen as an insult, and that had proved lethal in many a game of chance.

'Let's see, shall we?' Johnny said evenly, and then returned a glower from Ki Shing with an even stare that said, back off, cut me some slack, will ya? Easy, Johnny warned himself. Get that old poker face back on and don't rise to any bait. It sure has been hard to get that gold; don't lose it easy.

From the opening deal the play was helter-skelter, with Chung Wah going with any hand dealt and doubling the stake each time round. He didn't throw in his hand when the run was against him, and though he won a few hands at first, even raking in on pairs, straights, and three of a kind while the two other Chinese and Johnny threw in their cards, he soon began to lose steadily.

What the hell is going on here, Beamis asked himself. Wah's playing like a school-kid with a rich daddy. He had always respected Chung Wah as a very good poker player; now, as the piles of red and white chips before Wah began to dwindle and the others started to really rake it in, Johnny wondered if maybe the wily little player wasn't trying to give the come-on, getting ready for some really wild playing for high stakes.

It was when Johnny drew the three aces, two face down and one up, that he made his first big break of the night. Chung Wah and Ki Shing stayed in on the opening bids, while Quang Ho threw in.

Most poker players have a trait, Johnny had discovered, if you watch closely enough, a give-away habit which shows if they have been dealt a good hand. Quang Ho always pursed his lips slightly when he was looking at a really playable hand. Ki Shing was harder to spot when his luck was in, but through long observation Johnny had noticed that if Ki Shing had something really worth betting on he would stroke the tops of his cards from time to time with the forefinger of his left hand. Those two had been easier than Chung Wah to spot, but once the gambler had begun to relax in Beamis's company, Johnny had seen that when Chung Wah was really cooking he would give himself away – to Johnny that is – by holding his hand a shade higher, as if to guard it from the others' gaze, and he would look out, over his gambling house, towards the fan-tan and the white-ticket tables, as if bored with the present game.

Johnny noticed that Chung Wah was looking out over the crowded room right now, and he wondered if three aces would be enough to hold the other man. He drew another card and his heart gave a little leap as he saw it was the ace of clubs. Four aces. Chung Wah drew his last card and then held his hand up high and looked out towards the fan-tan table where the fat man with the pocked face was the banker, the *tan kun*, or 'ruler of the spreading out'. He was busy now throwing down the random handful of black and white button-shaped counters, clapping down the brass fish lid over them and waiting while the players around the table placed their bets as to what remainder would be left after the *tan kun* had divided the counters by four with the hook-ended wand that he carried.

Chung Wah caught Johnny watching him as he turned back, smiled and looked across the room again. 'This is one good place, huh, Johnny?' he said softly.

'The best, Wah,' Johnny agreed. 'Couldn't think of anywhere else I'd rather lose my money.'

Chung Wah did not have a good hand as Johnny had thought. He was looking out and thinking how much he was going to miss the place. He turned again to the table and threw in a large pile of chips whilst looking over to catch the fat man's eye, mouthing to him to bring more of them. He threw in a further pile of chips and raised the betting once more.

Johnny followed suit. What the hell. It was win or bust tonight. Shit or champagne, as they say. Chung Wah stuck in and the others folded. Eventually even Johnny grew nervous and saw Chung Wah, who spread the hand. Three kings. What the hell was going on? Three of a kind! Johnny shrugged to himself and raked in the chips. He didn't like to count in front of the other players, but he was now several thousand dollars up.

And so the night grew late. Johnny continued to win, and Ki and Quang did OK at first, until they both went in double-headed against Chung, who wiped them out, damn near, and that made them more cautious. Ki Shing began to shoot envious glances at Johnny, almost as if he had been specially selected by Chung Wah to receive his money alone.

'They tell me you're thinking of leaving town,' Johnny remarked to Chung Wah during a lull in play.

'Ah, news travels fast,' Wah replied, lighting a thin cigar. 'Yes, soon I shall leave. My work is almost done.'

'Soon we all go,' Ki Shing grunted. 'Your people drive us out, those they don't kill.'

'Now, they ain't my people, like you reckon,' Johnny said equably, 'and I sure as hell will be sorry to see you guys go.'

'It's happening all over the West,' Chung Wah said. 'They needed us for cheap labour, one time. Now the hard work's done they suddenly notice that we're different. We look different, we talk different hell, they even reckon we smell different, and they don't want us around. Those of us that won't go peacefully they string up, or burn alive like those two over in Arizona last week.'

'So where will you go?' Johnny asked Wah.

Chung Wah shrugged. 'Back to San Francisco, maybe. I want to go home soon, though, back to Kuangchung. Talk to uncle, see what new business we can stir up. The Chinese are the best business people in the world, Johnny. It's like food and drink to us.'

Johnny raised his glass. 'Well, I'm sorry for the troubles, Wah,' he said. 'I'm gonna miss you like hell. Luck, buddy.'

Chung Wah smiled directly into Johnny's eyes and raised his own glass. 'Luck, Johnny,' he said. 'Now, let's do what we're here for and play cards, gentlemen.'

Five

Johnny made it a rule never to quit while he was winning. If there was one other player who wanted a chance to get some back, then it was only right to give him the chance.

Which was why, at two in the morning, with both Ki Shing and Quang Ho out of the game and no other takers, he continued to play against Chung Wah, who was still gambling as recklessly as when he started the game six hours or so previously. The place was deserted, with only the barman and the pock-marked fan-tan *tan kun* clearing up, and Ki Shing and Quang Ho getting drunk along with Chung Wah and watching the game. A full house, tens and eights, gave Johnny the last of Chung's chips, and the Chinese gambler stared solemnly at Beamis for a while.

'Sold my mine today,' he said, apropos of damn-all.

'So I hear,' Johnny said, 'and to Clay Brunton, too.'

'What you driving at, Johnny?'

'He's no friend of yours. Hates the Chinese and makes no secret of it. You could have given me the first option, Wah.'

'Why you want my mine, Johnny boy?' When Chung Wah drank his English began to slip. 'Nothing in it for you.' Chung Wah giggled into his glass, and Ki Shing

33

laughed too, while even Quang Ho managed a dry smile. 'Anyway, that why I sell mine to that nice man, Mr Brunton. He hate Chinese. Thinks we're dogs, brainless dogs, that what he call us.'

'What do you mean, there's nothing in the mine for me?' Johnny said, feeling alarmed for Wah. 'You ain't played a trick on Clay Brunton, have you, Wah? He's a nasty bastard to cross, y'know.'

Clung Wah's eyes grew cold and slit-like, his face became a mask. 'Me too, I'm mean bastard, Johnny,' he whispered. 'Brunton killed a Chinese miner last week, him and his boys, bragged about it, too. So, he think I stupid, but I leave him with a hole in the ground, all he leave the miner, huh?'

'No, Wah, y'got to listen,' Beamis said, alarmed, but Chung Wah waved his hand to quieten him.

'I go soon, before Brunton know I gone,' he said. 'Then you watch the fireworks, my friend!'

'If you've done him down he'll come after you,' Beamis warned.

'He's got to find me first,' Chung smiled. 'Anyway, Johnny, tonight you got my mine.'

'How d'you mean?' Johnny asked.

The gambler, spread his hands out over the table, pointed to the chips. 'You cleaned me out, foreign devil,' he said. 'You have the money I got from Brunton for the mine!'

'God, I ain't too sure I like any of this,' Beamis said, feeling a little chill down his back.

'You wanna know just how I cheat Brunton, Johnny?' Chung Wah asked with a wicked grin.

'Jesus! No!' Beamis shouted without thinking. Chung Wah dissolved into helpless laughter, and even Quang Ho and the miserable Ki Shing joined in. They'd never seen such an unhappy winner, Ki Shing observed, though he spoke in Cantonese and didn't share it with Johnny, whom he referred to as 'the red-haired, long-nosed foreign devil'. Unlike Chung Wah, he wasn't joking. Racists are available in all colours, you know.

Six

The way the scam on Clay Brunton had worked was this way. The Run-Hog-Run mine (don't ask; no one remembered) had been played out for two years or more, and hadn't been all that great to start with. Dun Xei, an old Chinese guy, had traded a five-gallon keg of bad whiskey and a rusty pistol with a bust trigger for the mine with its previous owner, an itinerant Irish sot by the name of Kelly. By slow, painstaking methods looked down upon by the white man, such as carefully washing each boulder he removed and sifting through old spoil heaps, Dun Xei had won a fair living from the mine, even sinking a few coyote holes to try and find more gold, working his way down to the bedrock where the rich seams of gold would lie if there were any. There weren't, but Dun Xei was satisfied; he'd made enough to pay his return to the land of his ancestors and to buy a little pig farm there, and when he left, he gave the mine as a parting gift to Chung Wah.

Wah was in no hurry to sell; not that he thought that there was anything left down there, but he was a shrewd cookie, and he let the town know that he had a couple of guys working it for him, and occasionally he'd show a few pokes of dust or nuggets around, every bit of it stuff he'd won across his tables. Intuitively he knew there'd come a time when the old Run-Hog-Run would bring home the bacon, so to speak. Eventually it did.

Close by the Run-Hog-Run were the Magpie workings, one of the original mines in the area, belonging still to the two guys who'd wandered in with a mule and a shovel apiece and started the whole damn rush. Faulkner and Lewis were millionaires several times over and could have been living the fancy life back East if they'd had the inclination, but the stuff gets in your blood, and there was still a hell of a lot to get from that mountain, so though they had others digging and gouging in their places (most of it labour hired from Chung Wah), they were still back of the miners, driving them on, getting richer.

Then about a month before Clay Brunton came sniffing round, Chung Wah heard, casually over the tables one night, that Faulkner and Lewis had brought in a secret shift at the Magpie.

Now, the thing about a secret shift is not that no one knows that a secret shift exists in a mine when there is one. The secret is not even what the secret shift is doing (old man Faulkner, a miserable bastard even for a millionaire, once remarked that it amazed him how much harder it was to keep a secret down a godforsaken hole in the ground than it was in God's fresh air). A secret shift, after all, is only doing what every other man jack down a gold-mine should be doing, and that is, looking for, and getting, gold.

So, what happened with a secret shift was this: when the ore grew poorer in yield in a mine, or even ran out, then it was necessary for a team of skilled miners to go hunting for the good stuff. Of course, when it was found, the value of the shares in that mine would jump in value on the mining exchanges in San Francisco and Virginia City, and the astute owners who had held on to extra shares, or had even bought in during slim times, would sell at a tidy profit. Of course, if you could trust your exploration team to keep quiet for a while once they had found some more deposits of rich ore, then you could buy in shares in your own mine from frightened speculators who were worried that the mine was all played out, then sell off at a good profit when the mine was running at a peak. There was many a mine owner living high on the hog who had dug more precious metal from the pockets of ignorant but greedy folk back East than he ever had from a hole in the ground out West.

But to work the trick you had to be able to put together a good secret shift, as skilled and quiet about their work as assassins. And often as highly paid.

Faulkner and Lewis had been having a thin time at the old Magpie, and their secret shift had been working round the clock for weeks. Financial practice of the time allowed the directors of the Magpie to fund the considerable expense of the search by 'assessing' all stockholders, and the call for an extra $75,000 had gone out and been grudgingly met. It was incidental, of course, that the search would probably cost around a third of that price set, but, hell, as Lewis said to Faulkner, a man's got to live, and a lot can be hidden down a hole in the ground. And as Faulkner replied, who's gonna crawl a couple of thousand foot down, dive under twenty feet of water for a half-mile, to check that the new pumps we say are in place are really there, for example? Hiram Hardknot, clerk from Brooklyn, who'd just had to stump up the price of Faulkner's and Lewis's cigars for the next month? They thought not, and they thought correctly. So, the shareholders grumbled, but they paid up and hoped for better days and big dividends. Don't we all?

It had not escaped Chung Wah's devious little business brain, all of this, for he followed the stocks and shares in mining as much as anyone in town, where prospects and promises, indications and actual yields were discussed constantly, and it had been in the back of his mind to wait until the Magpie began to boom again, and then float some totally worthless and yet very profitable – to himself only, of course – shares in his mine, the Run-Hog-Run, on the market back in San Francisco, where a couple of his cousins could handle the actual issue and sale of bonds. Keep it in the family. It would stand to reason, in the minds of the usual buyers of mining shares that the Run-Hog-Run mine, right slap-bang next door to a successful mine like the Magpie couldn't fail to make money, and so it would. For Chung Wah.

But then had come the trouble in town, spreading as it was throughout the West between the powerful white men and the politically weak Chinese, and it looked, no it was certain, that Chung and his countrymen had to go while they still could, and soon.

So when the swaggering braggart Clay Brunton had sent for Chung Wah and made him an offer on the mine, Chung Wah began to see a way of making at least some money, a respectable profit, on the old, barren mine. Of course, it didn't do to look too interested, so at first he refused, said he was grateful for the offer, Mr Brunton honoured him by his attention, and all the other crap the white men expected from him daily in his dealings with them, but the mine was not for sale. Brunton was not a great one for patience or subtlety, however, and within a week a dead coolie had been found in the doorway of the Gam Saan. Following on the other lynchings

and beatings, Brunton's message was obvious, and he
sent Kirk Langley and a couple of the guys over to spell
it out.

'Accidents happen,' Langley said, with great original-
ity. 'That guy could have been you. Be at the mine by two
tomorrow afternoon. Mr Brunton would like to look it
over, take a few samples for assay, maybe make you an
offer. Be sensible this time.'

So Chung Wah had smiled and agreed, and bowed
and scraped the trio of thugs to the door, then he had
put into effect the plan he'd made weeks ago, when he
had first heard that Brunton had been asking about
ownership of the mine down at the Land Registar Office.
No one threatened Chung Wah. It had now become a
matter not of revenge, but honour.

Chung had ridden out to the mine in the company of
Yung Mo and Kao Li, he on his sway-backed, moth-eaten
old bay mare and the other two astride one donkey. The
effect was comic, and was meant to be. Who could have
suspected such a group of cunning and duplicity? Tied
round Chung Wah's back with a piece of rope was a
battered old shotgun, single-barrel. It looked like a scene
from a Chinese version of *Don Quixote*.

Brunton, Langley and two more sidekicks were waiting at the mine when they arrived, Brunton's bald dome,
which he seldom covered with a hat, making him clearly
distinguishable. Brunton glowered over at Chung Wah,
then turned his broad back on him, muttering something curtly to Langley, who came over, frowning.

'Boss says yer late,' he snapped, 'and y'can leave yer
hardware outside.' Since Brunton and the others were
armed with pistols, and weren't on their own property, it
seemed a mite overbearing to Chung Wah, but he smiled
and looked apologetic.

'So solly I late,' he said, in his best pidgin English, which he always reserved for the idiots among the white community. 'Need shotgun for lats and snakes.'

'He means rats and snakes, boss,' Kirk Langley called over to Brunton, who was moodily kicking shale down a spoil heap.

'I know, I know,' Brunton grated, and turned to swagger over. He was a medium-height man who made up for not being as tall as he felt a man of his importance should be by bullying and hectoring all those around him. 'Lats? Rats, man!' Brunton pushed his face close to Chung Wah, his spittle spraying the little Chinese gambler's face, his crazed, bulging eyes almost popping out, his trim little affectation of a moustache bristling with temper. 'You get 'em in every mine!' He turned to his men and said bitterly, 'Damn! I hate dealing with these people.'

And Chung Wah thought, you fool. With one upward chop of my hand I could drive your nose cartilage up into your skull and you would be dead before you hit the floor. Instead, Chung Wah bowed and mentally added on another thousand dollars he would ask of Brunton when the fool had been made to want, really want, the mine.

'Ah, yes, lats,' Chung Wah gabbled. 'Mine, he full of them, snakee too. My men no like workee down there, Boss Blunton.'

It was then that Yung Mo cut loose. He was an absolute treasure for what they had in hand that day, Chung Wah thought.

'No! No!' Yung Mo gibbered, pointing to the two piñon pine trunks which formed the props at the mine mouth, a crude door slung between them. 'Look like sticks of incense at funeral. Very bad sign. I not go down.'

Of course, it was all in Chinese, so Chung Wah

smoothly interpreted. 'You see, he thinkee lats bad magic. Also he see snakee in there - they worse than lats. He velly superstitious Chinaman, Missah Blunton.'

In truth, Yung Mo was one very superstitious man, Chinese or otherwise. He had come from a village way inland, and the peculiar beliefs of gods, ghosts, weather and nature spirits he held to confused even Chung Wah, so there was no chance Brunton would ever understand what the hell was going on with Yung Mo.

'I have to shoot lats and snakee, else men no come in mine, show you where best gold ore lie,' Chung Wah, said hefting up the shotgun and hamming the accent like hell.

'OK, but keep the damn thing pointing away from me, or I'll shoot you in self-defence,' Brunton warned. 'I ain't giving you no other warning, Chinee man.'

Chung produced a rusty key and played a while with the chain and padlock at the mine entrance. Finally, the door open, he produced a couple of lanterns from just inside the mouth of the mine, lit them and handed one to Langley, then shepherded a moaning Yung Mo and a very placid Kao Li down the tunnel before him with the white men in the rear.

Earlier in the day Kao Li had caught and killed a large rattlesnake on the mountain. Now he wore it beneath his shirt, wound round his waist. A shame it has to be thrown away like this, Kao was thinking. Marinade it in a bit of soy sauce, star anise and some rice wine, fry it with some coarse-chopped onions, make a very toothsome little snack. Ah, well, if it helped Chung get one over on the *gweh loh*. He trotted along behind his boss, ready to do his bidding.

Once inside the mine Brunton became like a kid at an Easter-egg hunt. He pulled a small geologist's hammer from his pocket and a load of linen bags and began to take samples from all around, writing on each bag whereabouts in the mine it was taken from. Chung Wah stood guard with his shotgun while Yung and Kao showed Brunton where they had supposedly taken the best ore from. Some he scraped or gouged off faces where, some days previously, Chung Wah had stood well back and fired his shotgun, driving into the rockface the fillings from his specially-loaded cartridges – pure gold dust. Brunton also paid close attention to ore heaps inside the mine which the Chinese miners assured him were rich in gold. They should have been; each pile had been watered earlier too with soluble gold chloride, ready for an unsuspecting Brunton, who knew as much about mining as a politician did about honesty, to sample for assay.

But the real clincher came when Brunton pointed to a low ridge in the mouth of one of the coyote holes old Dun Xei had dug years ago.

'Let's try here,' he said, holding a pocket compass, then in a hoarse whisper to his men, 'We're running in the direction of the Magpie here.'

Well, of course. Chung Wah stifled a smile. Stood to reason that if the Magpie could find gold, then there must be gold in this neighbouring mine. What a fool the man was.

Chung Wah gave Kao Li a surreptitious wink, then held his arm in front of Brunton. 'Please, you wait while coolie check for snake. He see big one here yes'day.'

Kao Li walked round the ridge of rock and dirt so that his lower half was hidden, and almost immediately gave out a shrill scream, at the same time throwing the snake to the top of the ridge, where it began to slither down.

Boom! went Chung Wah's shotgun, and the black

powder charge filled the mine, so that no one could see much. Yung Mo had gone, bolting for the light at the end of the tunnel. An old crone in his village had told him, the night before he set out for these cursed shores, that he would travel to a foreign land, where he would be eaten by a dragon. Well, she'd been having a bad day, and she'd always hated his grandaddy. Yung Mo didn't know this, and had believed her prophecy, and, hey, a snake was pretty near to a dragon, close enough for him. He was away, calling as he went down the tunnel on Yen Lo Wang, the god of hell, to spare him. It made a good distraction and Chung Wah was grateful.

'You waitee, please,' Chung Wah called out to the white men, and, loading up another cartridge which was packed with small gold nuggets, he discharged it into the ground around the snake, really messing up the rattler, to Kao Li's disgust.

Brunton walked up when the smoke had cleared and gingerly toed the snake away with his boot. He almost gasped with surprise when he saw the little nuggets gleaming up at him from the disturbed earth. That was the clincher. He had to have the mine. He was going to be one seriously rich man.

Seven

At last the poker game was over. Chung Wah and Johnny Beamis toasted each other once more with the last of the bottle of peach brandy. The gambling hall was almost empty; Quang Ho and Ki Shing had dropped out of the game, their stakes lost, and had waited to see which of the two men would finally win. The fat fan-tan dealer and the last barman had gone home and, as far as Johnny knew, they were the last people in the building.

'This guy you said that Brunton and his boys killed last week,' Johnny asked. 'You know anything about him?'

'He is – was – from my town,' Wah said. 'He has wife and children back in Kwangchow.'

Johnny took his original stake from the pile of chips, his poke of gold, and shoved his winnings toward Chung Wah. 'Can you see they get this, the woman and the kids?' he asked. 'I don't want this if it's got blood on it. Better they should live OK.'

Chung Wah nodded and took the pile of chips. 'His woman will get it all. You have my word of honour,' he said.

'You'd better make tracks if you've pulled one over on Brunton,' Johnny warned, 'or we'll be finding you dead in an alley pretty soon.'

45

Chung Wah smiled. 'Look for me here tomorrow night, and you won't find me,' he said.

'You're leaving so soon?' Johnny was taken aback.

'We've all got to go, Johnny. Every damn Chinese man in town. You don't come into town so often, or you'd have seen it, but every week now gangs of white men march through the Chinese quarter with flaming torches. Most of them wear masks or sheets. They're telling us if we don't go, they'll kill us, make no mistake about that.'

'Why?'

Chung Wah shrugged. 'Because we're different, and because they can't beat us down, like they have the Indians. Talk to Ki Shing here – he hates the white man – and he'll say it's because we're better than you, and, hell, he's got a point.'

Ki Shing broke in. 'We Chinese invented spectacles hundreds of years ago,' he said heatedly. 'We were using gunpowder while your people were still killing each other with clubs and walking round bare-assed. We invented printing while most of the white men were still illiterate savages. . . .'

'I've no argument with any of this,' Johnny said, holding up his hands. 'Far as I'm concerned, you guys are no different. . . .'

'You're right, Johnny,' Chung Wah said solemnly. 'I'm a man, no different from any other when you get down to the basics. I bleed, I love and hate, and when I'm wronged I'm hungry for revenge.'

'Yeah, it stinks,' Beamis said. 'God, I'm gonna miss you guys when you've gone. Hell, there ain't any honest card players in town but they come from heathen parts! It's wrong they can drive you out like this.'

'Know what the mayor said to me, when I went to ask

what would be done about the killings?' Chung asked. 'He said he'd looked in the town statutes and Territorial law books, and found plenty of laws against killing a man, but there was nothing against killing Chinese. Thought it funny, him and his councillors.'

Johnny shook his head. 'It ain't right,' he said. 'Seems to me this is a great, free country. Everybody should have the right to try and make a go of it out here.'

'Don't worry, my friend,' Chung Wah said, draining the bottle into their glasses. 'We Chinese are great travellers, and very adaptable. We'll go somewhere else, where our labour and brains are needed. We're great survivors, too.'

Johnny had grown maudlin with the drink, a thing he was not accustomed to. 'Still gonna miss you, Chung,' he said.

Chung Wah grinned and spread his arms wide. 'Tell you what, John Beamis,' he said. 'Let's have one more drink to old time's sake, and one more gamble, huh? A really big gamble!'

Johnny shook his head. 'I took enough off you tonight,' he said. 'Wouldn't be right.'

Chung wasn't listening. He leant back in his chair and bellowed something in his own tongue, and through a curtain from the rear of the building came a Chinese girl in a yellow, high-necked dress, carrying a bottle of peach brandy on a silver tray. Her raven-black, shining hair cascaded below her shoulders, and the yellow dress was slit high up her left thigh, so that when she walked a shapely bare leg showed. Johnny looked away quickly. It was not only bad manners to stare as he'd been doing at another man's woman, it could prove to be very dangerous, especially when that poisonous little creep Ki Shing was watching so intently, just looking for an insult.

'So,' Chung Wah said. 'One more drink and a big gamble, huh?' He clicked his fingers and snapped out an order, and the girl bowed meekly, stepped forward and poured the drinks then stood behind Chung's chair with her eyes lowered submissively. Beamis found himself staring despite himself, feeling the girl's humiliation for her. Almost as if reading his thoughts Chung Wah said, 'Don't mind her, Johnny. She is used to being treated this way. It is her position in life. It is best not to be too kind to her sort.'

'Well, it's your business – and hers, but we don't do it that way in America,' Beamis said, lifting the glass to his lips. He looked over at the girl again as he did so, and saw her look up from under her long lashes and direct a glare of absolute hatred at him. He looked away, thinking, what the hell?

'So, what's the deal?' he asked Chung Wah, who had already cut and shuffled the deck of cards in readiness for 'the big gamble' as he called it.

'Your original stake, that poke of gold in front of you,' said Chung, 'while I put everything here.'

'Everything?' Johnny asked, bemused. 'What do you mean, everything?'

Chung leaned back in his chair. 'Everything,' he said. 'The Gam Saan, fixtures, fittings, the lot. Like I say, all you see before you.'

Ki Shing hissed sharply in surprise. Clearly, the idea wasn't popular with him.

'But why?' Beamis asked.

'Why not?' Chung Wah replied. 'Tomorrow I'll be gone. Got to, before Brunton finds out what he's bought! The place is no good to me now.'

Ki Shing leant forward over the table and began to speak in Chinese to Chung Wah. 'We speak in English, out of respect for our guest, please, Ki Shing,' Chung said mildly, his eyes cold and flat.

'I would be honoured to give you fair price for the Gam Saan,' Ki Shing said humbly, his eyes on the table.

Chung Wah laughed. 'I know,' he said, 'but, consider, we Chinese have only weeks left in this town. Why, we may all be driven out tomorrow. Bad investment for a Chinese, this place, Ki Shing.'

'Then I will run it as partner for you,' Ki Shing persisted. 'I send you half the profits, whatever seems fair.'

'He's right,' Beamis said to Chung. 'Rent it to one of your own, or even give it to them. What's the point of this, Wah?'

Chung laughed. 'We're both gamblers, Johnny! You should know why, if anyone does. Simply for the fun of it. Come on, let's do it.'

Beamis thought awhile, then slowly grinned and shoved his poke to the centre of the table. 'You're on,' he said, then, as if he didn't believe it all, he asked, 'Everything'?'

In reply Chung Wah held up his right hand, palm outward, signifying that Johnny should wait a moment. Chung stood and walked away from the table, towards a back room. He walked into the darkness, and there was the sound of drawers being opened and muttered curses as Chung searched blindly, then the scrape of a lucifer being struck.

Johnny found himself looking again at the girl, what little he could see of her, as she kept her head well down. Once more she sensed his gaze, looked up and gave him a long, hate-filled stare. He looked away again, thinking, damn, what have I done to her? He changed tack, spent his time waiting for Chung's return by wondering what he'd do with a Chinese gambling hall if he won. The idea tickled him, even though he would have gambled for the Gam Saan if it were the last thing on earth a man wanted. He didn't worry what to do with such a place. After all, he could always lock the door and walk away from it whenever he wanted. That's what he'd do, he decided, give a party for all the Chinese gamblers before they left town, then lock the door and throw the key down in the street. Head up into the mountains, again, back to his mine. Johnny didn't like living in towns.

The girl surveyed Johnny from under her lashes. She breathed heavily but quietly. Never had she been so shamed, to be so humiliated, in front of a *gweh loh*. She had had little to do with his race before. In Kwangchow where she had been raised she had been kept well away from them, the lecherous foreign traders and the earnest missionaries, and here, in America, she had never gone beyond the Chinese community. All she had been told about the *gweh loh* had served only to make her distrust and fear them. Gods, but he's ugly, she thought, with his red hair, like the hair of a devil, his white skin scorched red with working in the sun all day. Look at his neck, red as a cockerel's comb! And his big nose, like the snout of a pig, with that long, red mousteche hanging down, like a dragon's fire. Ugly? She'd seen dogs that were better looking. In fact, she thought, he looked remarkably like a dog. She flared her nostrils and scented the foreigner. She caught the smell of sweat and tobacco. Dogs smelt better, she decided. That she should be brought this low, to be stared at by a barbarian, for him to witness her abasement. Chung Wah was a bastard to treat her so before someone who was not of their own kind.

Chung padded back to the table. In his arms he carried rolls of paper, account books, a spike with paid bills on it. He dumped the lot in the middle of the table.

'There you go,' he said, taking his seat and picking up the deck of cards. 'There's the deeds, signed and witnessed by a public notary, accounts, bills and invoices, list of takings for the past three years, bad debtors, and so on. Let's play.'

Johnny idly turned the heap of paper with one hand, and as he did so he unearthed a scroll, bound with red ribbon and with soot-black Chinese characters on it.

'I can't read this one,' he began, and as he held it up, the girl gave a gasp and began to speak swiftly in her own language to Chung Wah. Chung barely raised his voice, but whatever he said cut the girl like a whiplash. She lowered her head, but Johnny could still see that the girl was weeping silently, the tears running down her cheeks, unchecked by her hands, which hung limply by her sides in obedience to Chung Wah.

Again Ki Shing spoke, low and respectfully, but in Chinese again. For some reason he, too, seemed agitated by the sight of the scroll. Johnny did not understand what Ki had said, but the effect on Chung was as if he had had ice poured over him.

'Since you mention my uncle,' he said in English to Ki Shing, 'I will make you this offer. When I am in communication with him again, I will tell him about this night, and how you spoke up against me, his agent in this country. Then you can answer to him, if you like. Tell him you doubt his wisdom in sending me here. Is that what you want? I think not, since you are not speaking, but I will tell you this. The Gam Saan is mine, completely. It was my little ... hobby, bought with my money, not my uncle's. As for this. ...' Here he indicated the scroll: 'The reason I am throwing it in with the rest is simply because, when I am gone, I do not want it to fall into your hands. It was a present from my uncle, and it is mine to do with as I want, You and she would do well to remember that. Now be quiet, and think about what I have just said.'

Ki nearly filled his baggy little pants. Beamis had the pleasure of watching the man eat a lot of crow, silently. When he had finished speaking Chung flicked a finger in contempt at Ki Shing, who sat, head bowed, trying hard to become part of the background. Johnny didn't know who the hell this uncle was, but he clearly carried a lot of weight to be so frightening over such a distance.

'So,' Chung yawned affectedly, turning away from the craven figure of Ki Shing, 'do you have the balls for this game or not, my friend?'

Johnny said nothing in reply, but merely raised an eyebrow and nodded towards the red-taped Chinese scroll.

'She will read it to you, if you win, when I am gone,' Chung Wah smiled. 'Come, shall we play, all or nothing?'

'You're on,' Johnny said, thinking, what the hell. 'How do we do it?'

'Well, much as I have enjoyed tonight, time draws on,' Chung Wah laughed, oblivious to the girl's weeping and Ki Shing's discomfiture. 'Let's just make it five-card turnover, shall we?'

Johnny agreed and Wah dealt each of them a five-card hand, face down, then each man turned a card against the other. When the five cards were turned over Johnny had an ace high, against Chung Wah's king high.

Chung threw back his brandy and rose to his feet. 'You may not believe this, Johnny,' he said, 'but I prayed for this outcome tonight, as an omen. Now I know the gods have not deserted me, my ancestors are not angry, and my escape from this town will be successful. Good luck to you, my friend.' He extended a slim hand which was surprisingly powerful when Johnny shook it.

Before Beamis could think of what to say Chung Wah had neatly slipped from behind the table giving a stiff little bow to Ki Shing and Quang Ho. He paused by the girl to whisper in her ear, then walked to the front door of the Gam Saan and disappeared silently into the darkness of the night outside, leaving Johnny standing staring after him, astounded by the speed and finality of Chung Wah's departure.

For a while he thought that Chung Wah might return, so he stood aimlessly by the table, his hand on the pile of papers. Some minutes passed, during which time Johnny never spoke, nor did the Chinese girl make any move, but stood submissively behind Chung's empty chair. Finally Johnny stirred and said, to himself as much as to the other three round the table, 'Guess he ain't coming back. That's a hell of a way to leave, though.'

'The true adept moves as a fish through water,' said the girl, her voice making Johnny start. 'No man sees him come or go, nor does he leave a track by which he may be followed.'

'Say what?' Johnny asked, surprised that she had spoken to him, wondering if Chung Wah would return for her, or if she had made her own arrangements.

'She means that no stupid *gweh loh* will ever trap Chung Wah,' Ki Shing said scornfully. 'He is *kung fu*, great at hiding his true feelings and achieving his wishes. There is not a white man born who could defeat him.'

Johnny had never heard the expression *kung fu*, the name given to the secret fighting art of China, a method which used rigorous mental and physical training, more of a religion and an art than a technique. Kirk Langley hadn't heard of *kung fu*, either, but if he had been able

to speak, instead of staring sightlessly up from his shallow
grave directly below Beamis's feet, he would have come
down on the Chinese girl's side.

'Guess you know where to find him, huh?' Johnny
asked her. 'You'll leave town with him when he goes?'

The girl looked long and hard at Johnny. He saw at
first the look of hate she had given him earlier, then it
changed to puzzlement.

'You don't understand, do you?' Quang Ho asked
slowly. 'The girl is yours. You won her.'

'Now wait a goddamned minute here,' Johnny began.
'You mean. . . ?'

'The scroll,' Quang Ho said patiently, as if talking to
an idiot. He pointed to the little roll of parchment, 'The
girl is slave girl from Kwangchow, present from Chung
Wah's uncle in Canton to him. The scroll is like deed to
property. You won her. Now the girl is yours.'

Eight

'No, no,' Johnny shook his head in confusion. He'd won
. . . another human being? This couldn't be happening.
This was crazy.

'You don't want her?' Ki Shing was at Beamis's side,
plucking his sleeve. 'I buy her. I give good price.'

'For God's sake man!' Johnny exploded. 'You don't
buy and sell people!'

'She is property, not people. Look!' Ki Shing insisted,
brandishing the red-ribboned scroll with the soot-black
spidery symbols on it. 'I buy her from you, now.'

'What would you do with her, if I was to sell her to you,
huh, Ki Shing?' Johnny asked quietly.

Ki Shing made the mistake of telling Johnny, really
spelling it out, in case he didn't understand.

'Now, listen good,' Johnny said, after he had got hold
of Ki Shing by his shirt front and lifted him up so that
they were looking eye-to-eye, Johnny holding the fabric
of Ki Shing's shirt in a bunch close to the neck so that the
pimp had difficulty breathing properly. 'You walk out
that door now, and I'll try to forget you took me for
something as low as you. Say another word and I'll tear
you apart. Now, git!' He released his hold, and Ki Shing
fell to the floor, then scrambled up, rubbing his throat.

He slunk to the door, paused briefly to glare angrily at Johnny, then was gone.

'That's a bad man to cross, John Beamis,' Quang Ho said softly. 'You may be sorry for this night.'

'Yeah, maybe,' Johnny said sourly, reflecting that sometimes it wasn't as much fun winning as it was just playing. What the hell was he going to do now? He turned to the girl and said as gently as he could, 'You're free, missy, to go where you want. I ain't holding you to this.' He threw the scroll to the floor in disgust.

It was Quang Ho who picked up the scroll and placed it back on the table. 'It isn't that easy. . . .' Quang Ho began.

'Hell, course it is!' Johnny snorted. 'Watch this!' He picked up the scroll again and tore it in half, then threw it back on the floor. 'You're free,' he told the girl, who looked at him and then at the pieces of scroll on the floor.

'And where does she go to, now that she is free?' asked Quang Ho.

'Why, anywhere,' Johnny said exasperatedly, 'I don't own her. Why's it up to me?'

'Because you won her,' said Quang. 'Listen. In this town there are 'bout two thousand Chinese. Nearly all men. Ki Shing has five women at his . . . place.' He pointed to the girl. 'If she walk out now, that where she end up, or somewhere like it. Every Chinese in town know she is Chung Wah's slave girl. He disappear, you disappear, fine, then someone else take her. She have no place, no people, not safe without owner.'

Johnny scratched his head. 'How about you?' he asked the Chinese man. 'Won't you help her?'

Quang Ho jumped like he'd been stung. 'No, no,' he said quickly. 'Ki Shing would have me killed. Believe me,

Johnny, it is for the best that you take her. Why you think Chung Wah put her in the deal?'

'Damned if I know,' Johnny said.

'Because he is leaving town fast, travelling light. He is in danger because of trick he pulled on Brunton. Girl would mark him out in a crowd, so he leave her with you, knows you will look after her.'

'Thanks, Chung Wah,' Johnny murmured.

All the time he had been talking Quang Ho had been hopping from foot to foot and shooting nervous glances towards the door.

'This is not a good place, Johnny,' he said, wetting his lips. 'Ki Shing will be back with others to take girl, and Brunton will come when he knows he has been cheated. You should not stay here. Now I go. Good luck to you both.'

Both. Johnny let that one sink in as he watched Quang Ho bolt through the door. *Both.* What the hell could he do with the girl? Just leave her here and walk out? That meant Ki Shing would get her, stick her in his brothel, or when Brunton came sniffing around he would find her here, take his anger out on her, maybe beat her – or worse – to make her tell him where he could find Chung Wah. No, he couldn't do that. So why not ask her what she wanted to do, where she intended to go?

'Do you speak English?' he asked, turning to her, but she was gone. An open door, the one through which she had come with the brandy, showed the direction she had gone in.

Curious as to where she had gone and also interested to see what the first building he had ever owned – apart from the terrible old shack at his mine – looked like, Beamis stepped through the door and up a flight of stairs, with the moth-whisper of the girl's silk slippers moving through rooms before him, his way lit by candles in delicate lanterns decorated with golden tassels and lacquered in red and green patterns.

He stepped into one room, calling 'Miss', heard her feet in the room beyond that and hesitantly followed, wishing again that he'd lost that last hand to Chung Wah. He picked his way around the furniture of what was obviously Chung's parlour and reached the partly open door of what he could see was an opulently furnished bedroom, with a large, low sleeping-platform in the centre, covered with ivory silk sheets.

The sound of a cabinet opening and the hurried *clunk* of steel knocking against wood, of a scrabbling noise and the unmistakable sound of a shotgun being broken open to load it, reached Johnny's ears. Somewhere behind that door the Chinese girl was preparing to receive her new owner.

Johnny had not seen much gunplay, but enough to know that when someone is aiming to ventilate you with a sporting gun, it is unwise to make too easy a target of yourself. He gingerly reached out, tapped lightly with his knuckle on the door, then flung himself sideways to flatten against the wall, calling out again, 'Miss, are you in there?'

Boom! roared the shotgun in the confined space of the room beyond, and a large hole was torn through the swinging door, which flew outward with the impact. Johnny tried to melt his body into the wall and shouted something obscene which went unheard in the explosion, and as it died away his still-ringing ears heard *Ping! Ping! Ping!* as some small objects ricocheted around the room he was in. From the room beyond came the soft *phlug* of the shotgun being broken open and the sound of scrabbling fingers reaching inside the cabinet again for another cartridge.

Johnny's grandma, who was a bitter soul and not much good with kids, had always said that he was more than a mite slow in the thinking region, but he would have surprised her that night. One shot then the sound of a reload, even to a guy unschooled in the use of guns as Johnny was, can only be telling you one thing. The gun being used is a single-barrel sporting gun. No nasty little second shot waiting to spread you as you sashay quickly through the door.

Which is what Johnny did, at the double. To find the Chinese girl about to plug the barrel with a fresh cartridge and finish the job she was clearly aiming to do on him.

He knocked the gun up in the air, grabbing the barrel close to the trigger-guard, and with his free hand he gave the girl a strong shove, sending her flying over a low stool and on to the sleeping-platform. She rolled backward, affording Johnny a glimpse of shapely legs and strong thighs as the *cheongsam* she wore rode up. There was no time to admire the view, however, as she immediately jumped back over the stool and went for Johnny's face with her nails. Johnny grabbed both her wrists and held them tightly, so she aimed a swift knee up into his groin. He automatically moved his left leg to block, covering a man's most valued assets, but she scored a partial hit to the right, painful but not incapacitating. This was getting serious. Tears filled Johnny's eyes, but he hung on grimly. Who knew what other weapon she could snatch up to finish the job? Shit, she was lethal with just her bare hands and one knee! Don't for Christ's sake let her get that gun again!

'Let me go!' she screamed, spitting in his face. 'Pig! Bastard! Dog's ass!'

'Dog's ass?' thought Johnny. Where in hell did she get that one from?

She continued to struggle, her slender but strong little
body writhing against him, and Johnny felt a mite embarrassed that he could feel her through the silk dress,
moving against him. Damn, he hadn't been this close to
any woman, let alone a real looker like her, for a long,
long time, and it was having an effect on him, despite the
pain in his right ball. The girl's right hand came free as
he momentarily relaxed his grip, frightened of hurting
her soft wrists. Sharp nails gouged down his left cheek,
leaving bloody furrows.

Johnny lost it. He'd been shot at, spat at, sworn at,
kneed in the nuggets, now she'd drawn blood, all from a
woman whom he'd tried to treat decent and help out!
He was good and angry, and since his pa had always
taught him never to strike a woman he did the next best
thing – grabbed her by the front of her dress and shook
her till she was a blur, then when she was good and dizzy
he threw her backwards once more – harder this time –
so that she landed with a *whumph!* of expelled breath on
the bed. He followed her over and then leant down so
that his red and angry face was in hers, real close.

'I've had it with you,' he yelled. 'You lousy, ungrate-
ful . . .' he wanted to say 'bitch', but since his papa had
had strict rules also on swearing at womenfolk Johnny
finished off the sentence rather lamely with '. . . hellcat.

'What the deuce y'trying to do?' he demanded. 'Kill
me? Are you crazy or what?'

'I kill you, then kill myself,' the girl panted.

'What the hell for?' Johnny asked, puzzled as all get
out.

'You refuse to sell me, tear up paper which would keep
other men from me, then tell Quang Ho I am free to any
man who wants me,' she said. 'You pig, bastard, you
dog's . . .'

'Yeah, yeah, I got that last time,' Johnny said absently, then he suddenly realized what the problem was. The language barrier had nearly killed him. 'When I said you was free,' he said slowly, 'you thought I meant anyone could have you, free of charge?'

'That right,' the girl nodded. 'You not like this Chinese girl. Maybe think I ugly. That OK. I think you very ugly, like red devil. But you not give me to all men in town.'

'Free means something else as well,' Johnny said exasperatedly. 'Listen, willya?'

It took a while to explain, but when the girl realized how she'd flown off at half-cock, she lowered her head and Johnny saw a blush of embarrassment colour her cheeks. 'I sorry,' she whispered.

'Durn well ought to be,' Johnny grumbled, still shaken by his close brush with death. He turned and pointed at the door, which sported a hole in its centre the size of his head. 'Look at the door,' he began, but then paused as he did just that. 'What in the name of . . .' he said and walked forward to examine the hole more closely. Circling the hole, bedded in the wood and smeared around, was a halo of gold. Johnny touched it and some of the precious metal came off onto his calloused finger. Something crunched beneath his feet and he bent, picked up small nuggets of gold.

Johnny walked back to the fancy cabinet the girl had taken the sporting gun from. Several more guns, both pistols and rifles were in there and on a shelf boxes of varied ammunition. Separate from these were half a dozen cartridges which he could see had been opened and crimped back down again. Johnny tore at the end of one, removed the wad inside and tipped out the charge. Where there should have been lead shot were gold dust and small nuggets. He tried another. The same.

'So that's how he fixed Brunton,' he breathed. 'He salted the damned mine.' He looked across at the girl. 'Did you know about this?' he asked her. She nodded.

'He hide nothing from me,' she said. 'I his slave. Not important enough to lie to. And if I tell anyone . . .' she shrugged expressively. Johnny understood. 'I help him do it,' she said. 'I dig and bury, while he fire gun at walls. Chung Wah use two little bags gold he win from you one time.'

The irony of Chung Wah losing the money he had gained from the sale of the Run-Hog-Run, boosted by his salting of the mine with gold from Beamis's mine was not lost on Johnny. He didn't waste time laughing about it, however. He was too busy thinking what might happen if Brunton included Johnny in the list of folks to come calling on when he found out he had been duped. And there was nothing surer than Brunton finding out. He'd have an assay run on the gold, and what Chung Wah didn't realize, perhaps, nor Brunton – yet – was that the gold from Johnny's side of the mountain was quite different in colour from the gold they had been getting out of the Magpie and, when it had any left in it, out of the Run-Hog-Run Mine. Someone was bound to make the connection, seeing how friendly Chung and Johnny had been over the past two years. Oh, shit.

Johnny made a quick decision, the only one he could sensibly make. 'Listen, missy,' he said to the girl. 'There's trouble coming.'

Tne girl thought of Kirk Langley, lying below the floor-boards in his shallow grave, just waiting to be discovered. She thought, too, of the time she had seen Brunton swaggering down the main drag of town, cold-staring her with a lascivious leer, his usual escort of desperadoes sniggering at whatever it was he'd said about her. She thought of how little her life would be worth when Brunton started settling scores, and she nodded at Johnny's evaluation.

'Thing is,' Johnny said, 'if you need help to get somewhere, I'd be mighty pleased to help you. You can't stay here.'

Tne girl shook her head and looked down at her hands. 'There is nowhere I can go,' she said in a small voice. How she hated to humble herself before this man!

Johnny shifted awkwardly on his feet. 'Then, if you'd like to, y'could come with me,' he said gently. 'I haven't a plan yet, but the best thing is to get out of town while we can, put some distance between ourselves and Brunton. We can work out what to do later.'

The girl nodded. 'I come with you,' she said, then bit her lip and said very low, 'thank you for help.' It hurt to say, and she thought there had never been a time in her miserable life when she had had to sink so low as to thank a dirty, smelly, ugly *gweh loh* for his protection. She almost cried to think that she was alone, in a foreign, heathen land, where even her own countrymen either abandoned her or were a threat to her safety, where she had to trust this foreign giant, a man who was afraid himself. What would happen to her, she wondered. She wished desperately that Chung Wah would return. But he had gone. What had he whispered to her before he left? 'Stick with the *gweh loh*, if he'll take you. He is your only hope.' Then he had gone, the lousy, selfish pig!

What was the *gweh loh* doing now? He had found a tote bag and was opening the sliding doors which ran along one wall. Silk dresses hung inside, a rainbow of bright colours. He turned to her, said urgently, 'Quick, missy, pack some clothes. Whatever you need. We ain't comin' back, so pick wisely.'

Wearily she got to her feet and walked to a smaller cabinet stood against the far wall. 'Those too small,' she said over her shoulder as she swiftly selected from her wardrobe. She took out baggy Chinese trousers, a quilted cotton jacket, stout shoes.

'But don't you want any of these?' Johnny asked, bewildered, his hands unconsciously stroking the beautiful, expensive fabrics inside the wardrobe.

'No,' she said shortly, grabbing at a couple of silk dresses and packing them too, then pulling on the drawstrings of the bag. 'Where we go?'

'To my mine, first off,' Johnny said. 'I've got a shack there and some stuff I need to get. Then we better plan where to go. When Brunton gets round to looking for me, that's the first place he'll visit. You got a horse?'

'In stable, at back,' she said, thinking of the old, motheaten nag Chung Wah had left behind.

'Get it,' Johnny said. 'I'll go down the livery and fetch mine. I'll be back.'

The girl dropped her head once more. 'I afraid to stay alone,' she mumbled, clenching her fists till her nails nearly cut into her. She felt such shame that she had to confess her weakness to him.

'OK,' Johnny said. 'We'll get your horse, then go for mine. Best you keep hidden when we get to the livery.'

Without thinking, the girl began to take off her dress, then realized she was no longer with Chung Wah, who had insisted that she was to show no modesty before him.

'I must put trouser on to ride horse,' she said, and it was Johnny's turn to colour up.

'I'll wait outside the door,' he said. 'Hurry. It'll be getting light soon.'

Even as he spoke they heard from downstairs the sound of the street door to the Gam Saan being kicked open, of heavy boots tromping around downstairs. Rough voices could be heard, calling out.

'Hey!' someone shouted up the stairs. 'Anyone up there? Come down, now, or we're comin' up. We got the back covered, an' come down with your hands empty, hear?'

'That's Brunton!' Johnny whispered. He snatched up a handy little derringer from Chung Wah's well-stocked gun-cupboard and slipped it inside his waistcoat. There was no way he'd face Brunton without some sort of weapon. Sooner tackle a snake without a stick. 'You stay here while I go parley with him,' he told the girl.

'No, I come too,' the girl said firmly. She looked for a weapon to carry also, but Johnny shook his head. That Chinese dress was so tight there was no place to conceal a weapon. Durned distracting, too, he thought. Together they went down the stairs to face Brunton.

Brunton was waiting in the gambling room. A rough-looking *hombre* was at the foot of the stairs and followed them through, while another hardcase lounged against a wall behind Brunton. If Brunton was surprised to see Johnny there, he didn't show it, though he looked the girl up and down with an obvious leer. 'The Chink that owns this place, is he here?' he demanded, without any form of greeting.

'Nope,' said Johnny. 'Can't rightly say I know where he is.'

Brunton nodded, as if that was the answer he had been expecting. 'You in with him?' he asked Johnny with a sneer.

'No, we just play poker when I'm flush,' Beamis replied smoothly.

Brunton nodded his bald, bony head again. 'So I hear,' he said. 'I hear you got lucky tonight, as well.'

'That's right,' Beamis nodded back, 'though you don't want to believe everything you hear, Clay. Specially if a lying snake like Ki Shing tells you.'

The point went home. Brunton's face darkened. 'We'll see,' he said lamely, then went on the attack. 'Know what else he told me?'

'Oh, I got all night,' Beamis said, and grinned confidently at the thugs with Brunton, though his heart was moving a mite faster than normal, and the concealed derringer felt heavy and obvious as hell beneath his waistcoat.

'Well, that damned Chinee friend of yours sold me a mine that fair shone with ore,' Brunton said. 'Now I hear the double-dealing bastard cheated me over it.'

'No?' Johnny said with exaggerated surprise. 'Now how'd an idiot like him – and Chinese too – manage to do that?'

'Never mind!' Brunton snapped. 'But I'll tell you something now, boy. If that mine proves worthless at assay tomorrow, when I get the report on it, I'm coming back here, and I'm taking everything of his, and I'm gonna beat out of you where that Chink is. Cos, you know what I think?'

Beamis yawned and pretended to scratch his stomach, keeping his hand near the concealed gun. When he moved his hand again he kept hold of his belt buckle, ready to move it up to the gun as quick as he could move. Three against one was not good odds, he knew. 'Do tell,' he said. 'You sure been doin' a lot of thinkin', lately, Brunton.'

'I think,' Brunton said deliberately, putting his face close into Beamis's, 'that you and that Chink are in league. I think that this story about him losing this place and her . . .' he broke off and nodded in the girl's direction, 'is so much horseshit. He's gonna try and get out of town, and he's left you to look after the place for him – and his woman, though looking at your face, you ain't having much luck in that direction.' He nodded at the furrows down Johnny's cheek, and the two hired guns with Brunton dutifully sniggered on cue.

'Think what you like,' Beamis said evenly, though his colour had risen, and his breathing was coming a little faster with his temper. He nodded to the table, where lay the deeds and accounts books, all the other crap Chung Wah had left him. 'Fact is, I own it, all square and dandy, and above board.'

'Nothing's square and dandy when you dealing with that yellow scum,' Brunton said.

'Pity y'didn't think of that before you bought Chung Wah's mine,' Beamis said pleasantly, and Brunton's drink-reddened pop-eyes near bulged out of his head with anger. People weren't supposed to talk to a guy of his calibre like that.

Then Brunton did a stupid thing. He lunged for the girl standing behind Beamis, saying at the same time, 'Guess I'll take the whore with me. She'll know where the Chink is.'

Three things happened very quickly then. The girl raked her long nails down Brunton's outstretched hand, fetching blood. Brunton yelled for his thugs to get her, and as they started forward Johnny slid the old derringer out of its hiding place as smooth as a palmed ace and stuck it into Brunton's bulging gut, where it couldn't fail to kill if the trigger were pulled.

'Listen, you pile of shit,' Beamis said pleasantly, thinking at the same time, oh, hell, now I'm in deeper than I

ever been, 'the girl is with me, and she stays with me, got
that?' He looked into Brunton's pale blue bulging eyes
and saw there, with some surprise, real fear. He knew
then that the man was a coward, despite all his shout and
bluster, and that he would not try and call Beamis's bluff.
But Johnny knew also, sure as night follows day, that
there would have to be a reckoning for this.

It almost came sooner than either Beamis or the
somewhat colon-tight Brunton expected, for one of the
guys that Brunton employed saw his chance and took it.
He was a fairly unintelligent dude, but seeing his boss
was in trouble, and it was his own three meals a day and
found, he decided to think and act on his own for once.
He was standing behind and to the side of the girl, and
it was the work of a moment for him to step sideways and
bring a beefy left arm around the girl's neck.

'I got her, boss,' the guy called out, and to Beamis,
'drop your gun, or I'll break her. . . .'

He didn't get to specify the bodily part he intended to
fracture, for the girl decided she didn't want to play the
helpless female, and to the surprise of all the men
present she seemed to bend forward slightly, whilst pushing her well-formed little tush into the gorilla's groin. At
the same time she brought both hands up, grabbed the
guy's arm, and next news he was airborne. Not for long,
because the girl still held on to his wrist. She pulled hard
on his arm as he flew over her head and gave a loud
scream. Not loud enough, however, to mask the sicken-
ing sound of bones being broken under the stress of his
impetus trying to resist her grasp, nor did her scream
match his as she whipped him downwards to the floor
and then left him to grovel around beneath a table,
sobbing with pain and trying to get into the foetus position in the erroneous belief that the Chinee she-devil

couldn't get him again if he just made himself smaller.

As soon as Johnny had got over his surprise and could speak again he gave Brunton a dig with his dinky little derringer and ordered him to tell his remaining able-bodied henchman to drop his gunbelt on the floor. The hardware was followed by Brunton's, then Johnny gave the wounded man five to throw his gun over.

'Now,' Johnny said, 'you just sashay out that door and don't come back, or I'll plug you, I swear. I had enough of this fandango for one night.'

'Oh, this is just the start of it,' Brunton warned from the doorway, his courage returning with distance, blustering like a true bully. 'You've taken from me, Beamis, and I'll get even.'

'I've stolen nothing from you,' Beamis said. 'I want nothing to do with this.'

'I know you and your Chinee friend have put the fix on me over the mine!' Brunton shouted. 'Don't try to leave town till I've had the assay run tomorrow. I'll have guys watching the roads out. And I'll be looking for your friend too, tell him. And Kirk Langley. . . .'

'What's Langley got to do with it?' Beamis asked, mystified.

'I don't know yet,' Brunton said, 'but he was seen earlier, coming here, and he ain't been back since. I figure he's in it with you and that damned Chink. If you see him, tell him he's a dead man.'

In the silence of the room the Chinese girl gave a nervous giggle. Despite the tension the others stared at her in surprise. Since she had seen Kirk Langley and knew just how dead he was, she was the only one who got the joke.

In a mining town, where it is essential to keep up with what the next man is doing, little can be hidden from

one's neighbour, so just as Ki Shing knew that Kirk
Langley had visited the Gam Saan earlier that night
(though Langley had hoped darkness would conceal his
visit), so quite a few observant folk among the Chinese
community knew that Ki Shing had visited Clay Brunton
after his fall-out with Beamis, and that not long after-
wards, Brunton had come storming out of his saloon and
headed straight for the Gam Saan. It did not, of course,
take long for someone to drop the news into the ear of
Chung Wah, and even less time for Chung Wah to send
someone else after Ki Shing. Normally, he would have
done the job himself, and taken a grim enjoyment from
it, but he did not want to run the risk of being seen on
the streets, nor did he want the whole of the Chinese
community knowing that he was still in town. So he stuck
indoors with the folks he had taken temporary refuge
with, the giggling old Chinese lady and the old man with
the twisted leg and missing fingers, even though he
found the ancient couple tiresome company. From time
to time the old guy offered Chung Wah a toke on his
opium pipe. Chung Wah shook his head, but the old lady
took a pull now and then. When she drowsily made a very
improper suggestion and the old man started giggling
too Chung Wah smiled thinly and told them in some
detail what was going to happen to Ki Shing very soon.
They got the hint – he was his uncle's nephew all right,
they thought, smoked a bit more opium, and fell asleep.

Ki Shing wasn't so lucky. He had really upset Chung
Wah, and a little, oblique warning just wasn't going to be
enough for him. He didn't, however, have long to worry
about what was going to happen. He hadn't even
thought that Chung Wah would send someone after him,
he was so angry.

He was walking along the boardwalk that ran the

length of Jackson when he saw the guy in the black suit and wide black hat walking towards him. Taking the man for a *gweh loh* Ki Shing stepped down into the street. It was always best to give way. If the man was drunk or just hated the Chinese he was likely to abuse Ki Shing, or even push him off the boardwalk into the dirt. However as he came alongside the man looked up at him and Ki saw that the man in black was Chinese. Ki Shing shivered for some reason and hurried on, but as he turned into the Chinese quarter he glanced over his shoulder and saw that the man was now following him. Ki began to walk faster. Not far to his restaurant now.

He had his feet on the steps of the wooden building, his key in his hand when the first blow hit him. The man in black had got it wrong, possibly because he had had to reach up and then strike downwards with the little Chinese cleaver, so the sharp edge was deflected by Ki's shoulder.

Ki spun round, screaming, and this time the high-binder, the man from the Tong, did not miss. The sharp edge hissed through the air and caught Ki at an angle under the jawline, severing his jugular and windpipe with one blow. Ki Shing fell to the floor and scrabbled around briefly before he died. The man in black walked casually on, leaving Ki Shing as a warning to anyone else who thought Chung Wah could be messed with.

Back home in Kwangchow, when Uncle had decided to send Chung Wah to handle things in America, some-one who had learnt of Chung's weird predilections had dared to suggest that maybe Uncle was sending the wrong man.

'Listen,' Uncle had said, very quietly, 'Wah may be many things, but he always takes care of business. Always.' No more was said.

Everyone in the Chinese quarter of town who either saw Ki Shing lying in his own gore outside his place, dead like a dog in the street, or heard of it as the story spread like fire, knew. Chung Wah had taken care of business. He always did.

Nine

When the door had swung to behind Brunton Johnny quickly threw the bolts across and checked all other doors were shut. Then he ran upstairs for the bag containing the girl's stuff. He paused at Chung Wah's gun cabinet and checked one gun, a Colt .38 Lightning which seemed easy to his hand, and, scouting round further in the armoury's well-stocked depths found a matching holster, one amongst many, some hand-tooled, expensive.

'I didn't know Chung was given to wearing a pistol,' he remarked to the girl, who had followed him upstairs, dressed now in her baggy pants and black jacket.

'He like to dress up,' she said shortly.

'Yeah, everyone wants to look like a desperate character, huh?' Johnny said.

The girl shook her head, made as if she were going to explain, then just said, 'Wah very desperate character. More desperate than Brunton.'

Yeah? Johnny thought as he buckled on the hardware, so why's he running and Brunton looking for him, sister? He kept his counsel and when he was ready, he turned to the girl and said, 'You ready to trust me yet?'

73

'No choice,' she replied, shrugging her shoulders. 'I stick with you, that OK?'

'OK by me,' Johnny said, then he flushed and said in a rush, 'Look here. I want you to know, I don't mean to harm you, miss, or take advantage . . .'

'Advantage? What that?'

Johnny coughed embarrassedly. 'Never mind,' he said. 'Just so long as you know you're safe with me.'

'We not safe,' the girl said. 'Brunton want to kill us. You stupid?'

'No,' Johnny said, 'I meant that I won't try to . . .'

'Oh,' said the girl, as realization dawned. 'You mean you not try jump me?'

Where'd a nice girl like her get a mouth like that, Johnny wondered. 'You sure speak good American,' he said instead.

'Chung Wah teach me,' she said defiantly. 'But I know more than I tell him. I good listener.'

'I'll bet,' Johnny said, grabbing up the bags, the Lightning snug against his waist in its holster. 'Now, let's go.'

'Where to?'

'Out of town. It ain't safe here, with Brunton breathing sparks out of his . . . ears.'

'But he shoot us if we try to leave town,' the girl argued, nevertheless taking the heaviest bag out of Johnny's grasp and heading for the door. Chung Wah's training was dying hard.

'Yeah, and he'll shoot us if we stay,' Johnny said grimly. 'We can't just stay here and wait for him. . . .'

They were half-way down the stairs then, and the noise of the front window breaking came to them clearly, followed by the sound of several objects rolling and breaking, then the soft *whoof* of flames rolling out along the wooden floors, the crackle of the boards taking alight coming right after.

'Oh sweet Mary!' Johnny yelled. 'They've thrown in bottles of coal-oil!' He dropped the bag he was carrying, ran back into the bedroom and looked out of the window on to the street, trying to see where the fire-bombers were standing, waiting to shoot him and the girl down like dogs. He could not see how many were there. Brunton and at least two others, he guessed. As he showed himself at the window a rifle slug burst through the glass, narrowly missing his head. Johnny unshipped the shotgun from the rifle cupboard, thumbed in a cartridge and sprayed the street outside with twelve-gauge shot. Outside someone shouted in pain, then there was silence, no more shooting. They don't want to bring the sheriff, Johnny guessed, gonna wait for us to make a bolt out the back, and they'll be out in the alley there, waiting to put lead through us.

The girl tugged at his arm. 'Quick! Follow now!' she hissed, as the crackling of flames downstairs grew into a low rumble and smoke mounted the stairs. Johnny followed, coughing as they descended the stairs into thicker smoke. The girl turned and led him toward the back of the building, away from the flames, then just as Johnny thought that she was going to lead him right out into the waiting guns of Brunton and his boys she turned him to the side wall of the building and carefully began pulling at some of the boards. They slid out easily, revealing a low hole, blackness beyond.

'Where we going?' Johnny asked as the girl ducked down and passed through. She stuck her head back in.

'This the stable,' she whispered back. 'Come on – quick, now!'

Wondering just how many other bolt-holes Chung

Wah had, Johnny stepped into the stable. Inside, the old
bay mare was moving around in her stall and whiffling
nervously to herself as she caught scent of the smoke
seeping through the wall. The girl threw a saddle on the
nag and cinched it up, then she slung something over
her shoulder, a strap of some sort, and the rest of what
she was carrying went snug under her right arm, pointing forward. In the dark of the stable Johnny couldn't
rightly see what it was.

'What you got there?' he asked, as the girl moved
round to open the stable doors leading onto the street.

She showed him. It was a Remington twelve-gauge
sporting gun, its double barrels sawed-down till they were
damn-near stubs. A leather strap held it close into her
side.

'Quick! You get on horse. I follow behind,' she said
softly as the doors swung open so quietly Johnny
suspected Chung Wah had had them fitted and oiled to
be so silent. Beyond was semi-darkness and deep shadows
cast by a weak, cloud-covered moon. A man who had
chosen his spot well could have been standing nine feet
from them and he wouldn't have been seen.

For answer Johnny pulled the girl round behind the
horse and the wall. 'Listen,' he whispered. 'We go out walking. You stay close to the horse's side and I'll be up on the
boardwalk, looking out over the street. If anyone's there I'll
plug him and you jump up and ride like hell to Main
Street, then down it, not up towards the mountain. Savvy?'

'I stay with you,' the girl said, and before he could
argue with her, she had slapped the horse's rump and
they had walked out into the street.

Christ, but I'm scared, Johnny thought, thumbing
back the hammer on the Colt, his hands sweating on the
cherrywood grip. Then he heard, in the silence of the

night, two things. The first was the girl, very quietly sobbing with fear, keeping it low so that no one would hear her. The second noise he heard was the sound of a rifle being cocked. Under the overhanging buildings opposite, hidden in shadows, there was at least one man waiting to kill them.

Flame lanced out of the blackness, and Johnny swiftly but inexpertly fired two shots back. A voice called out a man's name in a warning that wasn't needed, and the rifle barked again. Johnny hadn't moved, and that was his undoing. Kneeling, peering in the darkness for his attacker, he hadn't realized that the flame from his own gun had given him away, and the man opposite had drawn a bead on him. He fired three times at Johnny in quick succession. The first shot smashed a window a good six feet to Johnny's left, the second splintered the boards in front of him, driving wood-splinters up into his face, the third took him in the side, close to the stomach, throwing him backward with a yell of agony as the burning lead passed into him.

He was a hard one, Johnny Beamis. Years of digging at the ground and blasting rocks for elusive specks of gold, or of sitting at gaming-tables, computing the odds against the riff-raff and desperadoes of a dozen mining towns, had taught him a hard lesson. Don't ever lie down on a deal.

Despite the pain he rolled to one side and snapped off another shot, then in weak moonlight he saw the girl emerge from behind the horse, her left hand held across her chest, her right arm in close by her side. There came the crashing roar of a sawed-off loosing one barrel, then the sound of a man screaming in agony. Johnny saw a dark figure roll off the board walk opposite, clutching his legs, which were drawn up to his chest.

Then the girl was kneeling by Johnny. 'You hit,' she said, a statement, not a question. 'Bad.'

'Hurts,' Johnny said, trying to struggle to his feet, feeling the blood running inside his shirt. He screamed and fell back. She half-lifted and half-dragged him to the horse, while he bit his lip, fearing he would faint. All the time he kept waiting for the next shot from the darkness to find him – or her, but none came, only the man on the floor kept screaming and cursing in pain at the buckshot which had mangled his legs.

Somehow she got Johnny on to the horse, then scrambled up behind him and urged the nag into a fair trot down out of the Quarter and into Main Street. There came a challenge on the outskirts of town. For answer the girl dug her heels into the nag's flanks and urged a swifter pace from it. A shot came winging at them from behind a shack, and the girl turned and blasted the shotgun in the general direction of fire. There came no answering shot, only the sound of booted feet running down the boards away from them.

Through his pain Beamis realized the men had gone running to fetch horses, to pursue them. They wouldn't be far behind, but he no longer cared. He wanted only for the pain to stop, and that could only begin to happen if the damned horse would halt and let him down. Shock had set in, and he didn't realize it, knew only that the pain was bad, but that he was drifting off to sleep. Soon all this would stop. . . .

The girl reached up with her free hand, the other holding on to the rein and supporting him in the saddle. She grabbed him by the short hair at the back of his neck and twisted it so that he jerked awake with the sudden stab of pain. Then they heard the sound of hooves far behind but gaining.

'Quick,' Johnny gasped. 'There's a dry wash runs alongside the road here.'

'What is wash?'

'Never mind,' he said, sawing at the horse's neck with his left hand, sending waves of pain through his right side where the bullet had entered his body. It felt like it was still in there.

The horse turned and slid down the side of the road, into the flood-water course that barely hid them. The girl stifled a scream as the horse threw them to one side and both fell onto the hard-packed soil and rocks. Johnny fainted with the pain.

When he came to again he heard horses thundering along the road, three he guessed. The girl was speaking rapidly in her language, something with the tone of an entreaty. She was praying to Kuan Yin, who was burning even now in the flames of the Gam Saan, along with the other images of gods Chung Wah had prayed to. She felt sorrow at the loss of Kuan Yin, though she hadn't had a second thought about Kwan Ti, for he was the god of war and would gain strength from the flames. The thought occurred to her that he might even be thoroughly pissed with Brunton for setting fire to the Gam Saan and destroying one of his images, and would wreak terrible revenge on him. Then another thought came to her, as she prayed to Kuan Yin, that maybe Beamis was an emanation, a projection into the world of humans, of Kwan Ti or Kuan Yin, since he had stood up for her against Brunton, had fought for her and saved her. If so, Johnny could use some help right now. She prayed harder, and as she did so the moonlight was extinguished by thick cloud, masking them where they lay, so near to the road.

The riders charged past, so close that Johnny and the

girl could hear them shouting to each other.

'Where'd they go?'

'Not far ahead now.'

'Langley with them, or the Chink guy?'

'Nah, just the Chinee girl and Beamis. Reckon it was him, the long streak of. . . .'

And they were gone, past them and into the night.

'They'll be back soon,' Johnny said, on his hands and knees and trying to rise, faint moonlight reflecting on his blood-soaked shirt. She knelt by him, opened the shirt and quickly tied a whole silk dress from her bag, tight around his belly and back.

'Now you wear my dress,' she tried to joke, as he slowly tried to rise.

'You'd look better in it,' he groaned. Somehow he got to his feet, mounted the horse with her assistance.

'Where now?' she asked from behind him, holding him in the saddle.

He just grunted and nodded forward, down the wash. Further down, the way flattened out, was joined by several other washes. Johnny urged the horse along the third wash and started to angle up over the shoulder of the mountain. He'd prospected up there some years ago, found no gold then, just something which might save their lives, at least hers, if he could just hang on a mite and not die before he got her there.

Ten

He'd been so careful and still he ended up nearly being shot by a stray bullet that came winging its way up Main Street, burying itself with a soft thunk in a wooden upright outside a saloon. The wizened old coolie thanked his gods and hastened up Jackson Street into the heart of China Town. Behind Chung Wah's Golden Mountain gambling den, now well ablaze, he skirted the man who moaned and scrabbled in the dirt, clutching his legs. The old man crossed the road, looked around carefully, and then finally, with a speed that belied his years, dived inside the mouth of a dark alleyway, and ran quietly down it to the end. There he knocked softly on a low door, identified himself, and was admitted, though there was a slight wait whilst the light inside was extinguished.

His name was Ling Weh, but the white miners, when they were not cursing him, called him John Chinaman, because they could not be bothered, or thought it beneath them, to speak his Chinese name. Ling Weh was a cleaner at the Magpie mine. He was also a close associate, from way back, of Chung Wah, though the two men had thought it best that that fact was not widely known,

81

even among the Chinese in town. Chung Wah had
people everywhere.

An unfortunate accident at his birth, which had been
a difficult one, had elongated Ling Weh's lower jaw, so
that it thrust forward, and gave him the look of a simple-
ton. Ling Weh was anything but. He had found through
working with *gweh loh*, however, that it often paid to let
others think he was stupid, and Chung Wah too had
encouraged the deception. He had also counselled Ling
Weh to feign deafness and a very limited knowledge of
the English language, although Ling Weh spoke it almost
as fluently as Chung.

Chung got him a job at the Magpie, telling the boss
there that Ling was fit only for swamping and light
labouring jobs, and before long Ling Weh was swamping
out the superintendent's changing room, cleaning his
working boots and mine clothes of the mud that stuck to
them when he was in the lower levels.

The secret shift, too, used the same changing area,
and the night that the Gam Saan was set ablaze, they had
come up, as close-mouthed as usual, but Ling heard the
superintendent joshing them. The superintendent had
been down in the sealed-off lower level the secret shift
had been working in for the past four weeks, searching
for the elusive vein. Speculation was rife, not only in
town, but on the exchanges where the stocks in gold and
silver were bought and sold. Ling Weh succeeded where
others failed, simply because he was overlooked, not
thought important enough to be worthy of suspicion.

'We'll have the assay by Monday, boys,' the superintendent said as they left, he toting the sample bags.
'Come in as usual in the evening to keep everyone guess-
ing, but don't do any work. I'll be down to tell you the
good news, I guess.'

The miners were all on for some shares in the stock, bought for them by Faulkner and Lewis, the owners of the Magpie Mine. These were bought for them at the low price the stock fetched when many were saying the mine was played out, to be sold later, when the new ore was being worked and the stock was priced high on the exchanges once again. The guys on the secret shift looked pleased as they left.

Ling Weh quelled his own anticipation and began to clean the superintendent's boots of the mud which had adhered to them whilst he had been inspecting the new drift the secret shift had driven. Once Ling Weh had done this he put it in a little pile on a copy of the local paper, the *Thunderer*, not noticing that as usual the editor was fuming about the threat posed by such as Ling Weh and his 'heathen' countrymen. Then Ling Weh turned his attention to the superintendent's jacket, shirt and overalls. These he scraped with a blunt knife, adding the mud to the pile on the paper, turning out the pockets also and adding loose samples of ore the superintendent had picked out as he worked. Finally the Chineseman took the old battered felt hat of the super's and scraped that, which gave him a sample of the roof of the drift. When he had finished, twenty minutes later, he rolled the whole caboodle into a large ball. He now had a sample of the average content of the new drift, and hummed happily to himself the tune of a song about the old Pearl River back home. With any luck he'd be seeing it soon, with a hell of a sight more cash in his pocket than he'd had when he'd sailed downriver, heading for America.

As Ling Weh left the mine with the ball of mud in his baggy jacket pocket a guard spat at him as he passed through the mine's outer gates. Ling bowed and told the guard that his mother had been a bitch who mated with a monkey – in Cantonese, of course – and made his way down the track to town.

There was shooting as he came down Main Street and turned into Jackson, so he hid in the doorway of a saloon, crouched so low down after the bullet nearly hit him that he didn't see who was mounted on the old nag which cantered past in the dark. Nothing apart from his own life was as important as getting the ball of mud to Chung Wah. The man lying wounded on the street, calling for help, did not concern him – he was white, after all, had probably been in on the burning of the Gam Saan. As for the blazing building, well, Chung Wah was too clever to have been caught inside, and anyway, he was always waiting in the other place for Ling Weh's report when he came off shift. Tonight, they'd both be busy with the ball he carried.

A tap on the door, a quiet challenge from beyond, then the darkened door opened just wide enough for Ling Weh to slip through. It was the crippled old man who had opened the door. Chung Wah stood to one side, holding a shotgun cocked and ready, just in case Ling Weh had brought company.

'You OK?' Wah asked.

'Yeah,' Ling Weh answered, then, 'What's happening over at the Gam Saan? It's alight.'

Chung Wah sidled over to a window, lifted a dirty curtain and peered out, holding the shotgun carelessly by his side.

'Beats me. Been burning for a while now.' He shrugged. 'Lost it in a poker game to Johnny Beamis. It's his concern now. Sure hope he gets out. You got the stuff?'

For answer the swamper held up the ball of mud and

grinned. 'I reckon we are in business,' he said to Chung Wah.

'Come through,' Wah said, turning from the window and making for a back room.

'Reckon we're safe?' Ling Weh asked uneasily, looking at the red glow that was shining down the alley and lighting up the curtains. 'Wooden buildings, a fire soon spreads.'

'I checked the wind,' Chung said. 'It's blowing towards the *gweh loh* section of town.'

'Serve the bastards right,' said Ling Weh, nodding pleasantly to the old couple in passing. 'They probably lit it to burn us all out.'

Even as he spoke there came the distant sound of fire bells as the volunteer fire-fighters galloped down Main Street with their fire tender. Blazing embers, carried high on hot updrafts from the Gam Saan and adjacent Chinese-owned buildings were now raining down on the white section of town, and a lot of the town would be ashes before dawn finally broke. More would have been flattened, pulled down deliberately, to halt the course of the blaze. The Chinese would blame the whites, saying it was deliberate, to drive them out of town, and the whites would blame the Chinese, saying they were primitives and couldn't even be trusted with fire. Those who knew, Clay and his boys, would say nothing. They daren't.

In the next room Chung Wah had set up a small but effective assayer's lab, with crucibles and grinders, chemicals and retorts, fine-balance scales to measure the gold produced from his final processes. The assay took a while, but when they'd finished, Chung was grinning. 'Better even than the last test,' he said. 'They've struck very high grade ore. Time we were getting back to 'Frisco.'

'I was going to suggest that,' said Ling Weh. 'Don't want to worry you too much, but when I came by the Gam Saan, there was a *gweh loh* lying on the street. Been shot in the legs.'

'And. . . ?' Chung asked.

'He kept calling out for someone called Clay,' Weh said.

'Yeah . . .' Chung said, stepping back from the table he'd been weighing the gold at. 'I was expecting it. Ki Shing was shooting his mouth off to him earlier. Seems to have really done a number on me.'

'The black snake!' Ling Weh spat. 'He ought to be. . . .'

'Don't worry,' Chung said absent-mindedly. 'It's being taken care of right now.'

'So what did you do to Brunton to get a hair up his ass?' Ling Weh asked. He prided himself on being able to use American colloquialisms as well as Chung Wah.

Chung Wah told him.

Ling Weh whistled. 'That makes it more difficult for us to get away,' he said, then laughed. 'Well, you, anyway,' he said. 'He'll be looking for you, not me, when that morning train to San Francisco pulls in.'

'And we'll walk out right under his nose,' Chung said. 'I've had something planned for a while now, in case either Faulkner or Lewis guessed what we were doing at the Magpie, but it'll do to get me out of town safely.'

'What about Beamis?' Ling Weh asked.

Chung crossed the room and peered through a window. At the end of the alley the buildings were burnt out, heaps of glowing embers. People scurried by, shouting in Chinese, carrying items they'd saved from the blaze. 'If Beamis was in that, he's dead. If Brunton got him, he's dead,' Wah said, then shrugged. 'Still, he's a gambler, and he's got the girl with him. They'll make their own luck.'

Eleven

Johnny's luck was holding, though right now he didn't feel lucky. As dawn broke they had ridden up over the shoulder of the mountain. They had not been followed as far as they could tell, though apart from pausing to check Johnny's wound was tightly bound still, the girl allowed no rest. Now they began to descend slowly, following a trail that was trodden rarely by anything larger than the native mountain goat, but the old nag had sure feet and since people had stopped shooting at her she had settled down. Often the girl walked ahead, holding the reins and guiding her. Johnny leant forward over the horse's neck, just hanging on and trying not to scream when the pain in his side grew too much to bear. He truly thought that he would die soon, but each mile he hung on took the girl a mile nearer safety. Where they were heading took some finding. He didn't want to leave her out here, prey to any passing desperado.

Eventually, as the sun strengthened and rose to its zenith, they came down off the mountain path into a high valley. Down the steep sides ran little streams in places, and these had been channelled and directed so that they had left their natural courses and, wandering over the flat area, had made of the valley floor a boggy swamp, through which the horse ploughed noisily and slowly, each step having to be taken with care. The girl could see beyond the swamp the narrow mouth of a canyon which snaked back into the mountain beyond the swampy stretch of water. Johnny whispered for her to take the horse forward, slowly, toward the canyon mouth, and she led it carefully through the water, sometimes knee-deep, stumbling and splashing. Reaching higher ground eventually, she urged the horse up on to it, away from the swamp, among jimson-weed and juniper-berry and sagebrush. Every step the horse took its hooves snagged on threads twined between the bushes, each connected to suspended cans, Borden condensed milk and Chase and Sanborn coffee-tins, which clanged and clattered, announcing their presence to whoever lived up the canyon. Clearly not a person who liked visitors to arrive unannounced.

The girl stood by the horse's head, unsure, frightened by what might wait ahead. Was this what the damned *gweh loh* had led her to? Half-way round a mountain, along precipice edges, picking her way between great banks of scree to this? She began to doubt Johnny, said a silent prayer to Kuan Yin to save them both.

From his slumped position on the horse's neck Johnny peered through pain-racked eyes and croaked, 'Call him.'

'Call who?'

'Call Al. We're here, safe.' And he fell, unconscious from the horse to the soft earth, his last thought being that he could die now. He'd got the girl out and she'd be OK, though he'd like to have met up with Brunton. He'd have. . . .

The girl started round the horse to Johnny's side, and as she did so a man rose from a nearby clump of arrow-head, a rifle held steady on her.

'That Johnny Beamis?' the man enquired.

The girl nodded, wished she hadn't tucked the shot-gun away in one of the saddle-bags.

'You shoot him, or you his woman?' the man asked.

She thought about that one. Her skin crawled at the thought of being the barbarian's woman, but if it helped her situation. . . . She lowered her head. 'I am his woman,' she muttered.

The man nodded, laid his rifle down, knelt over Johnny, began unwrapping Johnny's wound. She knelt at one side, looking in clear daylight for the first time at the horrid, purple, oozing mess. She felt sick, but fought it. Please Kuan Yin, she prayed, don't let the *gweh loh* die. He's ugly, foreign, and a worthless gambler, but please let him live, don't leave me out here, miles from San Francisco and any chance of getting back to China. Don't leave me out here alone with this . . . wild man.

'I'm Al,' the man said over his shoulder to her as he worked. 'I live out here.' He nodded back up the canyon.

It looked like it. Back in China there had been hermits in the mountains, following the teachings of Taoism, living for ever, people said, on a secret diet of roots and herbs and tiger-bone wine. But this one took the prize for crazies, for sure, she decided, looking at his antelope-hide trousers and shirt, his deerskin moccasins and his great, grizzled beard which seemed to spring out at all angles from his face.

She wondered what would happen to her if Johnny died. She might be safe right now, while she was 'Johnny's woman'. But if Johnny died, as it looked he might, what happened then? Would the hairy giant of the mountains just inherit her, take her over like a piece of property? She couldn't, not with him. Oh no! For God's sake, Johnny, don't die!

'We got to try and save him,' she said to Al. 'Please.'

'I can try,' the hermit said doubtfully. 'It's mighty close to being a gut-shot. Bullet's still in there and he's lost a lot of blood. He ain't in good shape, lady.'

For the first time since she had come to this godforsaken country the girl wept openly. Chung Wah would have despised her, maybe even have slapped her face and told her to stop, but Al was immediately all awkward concern, tried to make out Johnny wasn't as bad as he'd said, and she began to realize she had misjudged him for an uncouth beast. Al ran off through the bushes and came back with a piece of old canvas and two poles, out of which he fashioned a rough stretcher, on to which they rolled Johnny. Together they carried him slowly and with much effort up the canyon.

They passed through rows of beans and corn, with green vegetables growing beneath in the shade. As the mouth of the canyon closed around them there were hens, in coops cut out of the solid rock or scratching round in the dirt around them. Al's home was just beyond, a one-storey adobe, built into one side of the canyon. It was shaded from the hot sun by a *ramada*, a veranda with low lattice screens woven from fibres of the ocotilla cactus which grew in the desert below. From beams of the *ramada* hung *ollas*, large clay pots full of water, which evaporated slowly through the clay, cooling the remaining water and making the air beneath the *ramada* much more bearable.

Inside the house there were just two rooms, a storeroom and sleeping quarters which consisted of a large, rough bed set on a dirt floor. As they carried Johnny through the girl saw bare white walls with the odd weapon, a rifle, a brace of pistols, hanging here and there. Small windows set in deep embrasures gave on to the whole of the canyon, and it was clear that Al had built the house with an eye to defence as well as shelter.

They laid Johnny on the bed. He did not stir. He was deathly pale, and even the wound had ceased to bleed. He could be dead now, she thought in panic, and put her ear close to his mouth. A slight exhalation told her life was still present.

'OK,' Al said. 'We got to get ready. I'll heat the water and get some bandaging and stuff. You wash up and prepare yourself.'

'What for?'

'That bullet's got to come out,' Al said, pulling a slim skinning knife from somewhere. 'And there's only us to do it. You going to have to help, your hands are smaller than mine, can get right inside that wound. You any good at cutting and probing, huh?'

There was no answer. She had fainted away.

Twelve

Brunton considered sending two guys after Johnny, but his anger was directed towards Chung Wah, and he needed every man he had, specially after Kirk Langley had defected, and the Chinese bitch had shot Mac in the legs. She'd pay for that when he found her. Screw Beamis. He was most likely dead by now, anyway. Mac had shot him, all right. But he had to find Chung Wah and Langley. They were the guys who'd worked it over on him. He wasn't quite sure just how they'd done it, till Soapy Smith, one hell of a con artist himself, had told Brunton, pitilessly and publicly, just how the salting of the mine had been done. That was one he owed Soapy, and he'd settle the score with him once he'd dealt with Chung Wah and Langley. They were in town still, he was sure of that, and they'd only leave horizontal, dead, in a box apiece. Before he killed Langley though, Brunton promised himself, he'd make him eat dirt. He had no inkling that the guy had eaten enough already to make him gag if he'd been able to. . . .

After the total balls he'd made of the fire-bombing, Brunton had beat a hasty retreat and made a great show of helping limit the fire through the white business area. Even so, two blocks of wooden stores, saloons and eating-houses had been totally razed to the ground, two more blocks extensively damaged, and three lives lost before the flames were out. Brunton had talked up the fact that it had been started in Chinatown, 'by those damned heathens', and all right-thinking men in town were determined to drive the Chinese out for good and all. If a few of the yellow devils had to die, well, so much the better. Brunton patted himself on the back for sliding out of discovery as the real arsonist, and plotted his revenge.

First, to catch Chung Wah and Langley. He posted a man at each end of town, with a good look-out over the surrounding countryside, then he put four of his men on the station, since he thought Chung Wah might try to escape to 'Frisco at the earliest chance. First train through was at eight. Brunton himself was down at the railway depot for seven, looking back into town, when he saw them coming.

Not the men he was looking for, not that he could pick them out, but a huge throng of Chinese, their worldly goods on their backs or wrapped in meagre little bundles, quietly and with no displays of emotion, leaving the town for ever, coming to catch the first train out. Nearly three-quarters of their section of town had been burnt. They had lost ten lives, but it was not worthy of mention in the next issue of the *Thunderer*.

They were considered less than human, a necessary evil which had built the railway there, sunk the deep mines and laboured in them when there were no others to do it. Now? Well, they'd been paid, hadn't they? Time for them to go back to wherever they came from and stop taking bread from the mouths of true Americans, those who'd come from England and Ireland and Germany and Sweden and the steppes of the Ukraine, amongst other places. Guys whom God in His infinite wisdom had made white, and, therefore, acceptable in His eyes.

'What the hell is this comin'?' Whitey Guttridge asked his boss, but Brunton too was gazing slack-jawed at the oncoming throng. The other three guys he'd brought down to look for his prey drifted over to watch.

'They leavin',' Whitey finally decided. 'We druv 'em out. Hey, ain't that somethin'?'

Brunton scowled. How to pick out one Chinese guy in this crowd? It wasn't going to be easy. He finally decided that among all these Chinese it would sure be easier to pick out Langley, and he'd either be with his Chinese buddy, or could be tortured into telling where Brunton could lay hands on the cheating little rat. He split his men up again, and as the horde shuffled silently on to the platform the thugs began walking up and down the line, staring into each man's face. The Chinese kept their eyes down or averted. They knew how the land lay, and didn't want to finish up the target of a lynch mob.

Back of the queue came Mother Chu, the leper nun, a strange figure in her yellow robe and great crucifix, her bell ringing as she swung the staff to which it was attached, painfully hobbling along, her dark veil hiding her face. The old guy with the missing fingers was with her again, but carried no collection box. This time an old woman was accompanying them, and she hefted Mother Chu's baggage.

'Stay away from them,' Whitey hissed to one of the searchers. 'I reckon they pure rotten with that leprosy.'

The old woman bought three tickets and the party hobbled down the platform, even Brunton stepping well back in case some sort of infection followed in their wake.

Looking at the Chinese gathered on the platform,

patient, accepting, made Brunton uneasy. These people had made this place. Now, despised and beaten, they were leaving, their place in the dream denied them. He had driven them out, had beaten and killed them, burnt their homes. He had triumphed. He liked that, except. . . . One of them had bested him, sold him a worthless hole in the ground for . . . he did not like even to think how many thousands of dollars. All he possessed, all he could borrow, he had paid for the mine to that . . . Chink. He had told no one in town just how much. The only people who knew were Chung Wah, Langley, if he really was in on it with Chung Wah – oh, yeah – and maybe the gambler, Beamis, and his whore. Well, he'd kill them all. Show the whole town it didn't do to mess with Clay Brunton, no sir.

The train pulled in a few minutes before eight, and the throng scrambled aboard, packed tight in each carriage. Except the caboose in back, which the conductor turned over to Mother Chu and her party, seeing that no one wanted to travel with them, even the other Chinese, who seemed even more frightened of her, their fear tinged with quite a lot of respect.

Standing on the platform, angry, frustrated, Brunton felt there was something not quite right. He could not put a finger on it but he knew without knowing how that Chung Wah was on that train. He grew angrier with himself, but the hunch grew and grew till it rode him like a jockey. As the engineer came out of the depot and swung aboard the loco, Clay turned to Whitey.

'Ride the train for a few halts,' he ordered. 'See if the little rat or Langley sneaked aboard while we weren't looking.'

'They couldn't have, boss,' Whitey reassured him. 'They ain't on that train, that's for sure.'

He was startled by the ferocity of Brunton's reaction. 'Just get on the goddamned train, 'fore I put my toe up your ass to help you,' Brunton shouted, and Whitey, with a startled look at Clay's face, tight with anger, gave an almost imperceptible shrug to the other guys, as if to say, what the hell, humour the mad bastard, and climbed aboard the first carriage behind the great black locomotive.

The engineer rang the bell, the conductor shouted, 'All aboard!' to a platform that was empty save for Clay and his henchmen, and the train slowly pulled out of the depot.

Brunton took his hat off, wiped his bald dome, which was wet with sweat. Hell, he was losing it for sure. Forget Soapy Smith, even his own men were beginning to lose respect for him. Only way to get it back was to find that damned heathen and Langley and kill 'em, slow and nasty. But first, you got to find 'em. He turned on the three men remaining.

'Come on,' he said. 'Let's go take a walk round town. If they ain't on the train they got to be there.'

'Everybody's got to be somewhere,' one of the guys said, in an attempt at humour. One look at Clay's face told him that a joke right now was as welcome as a fart at a funeral feast. He turned and walked away, back towards town, but bravado or just plain dumbness prompted him to make some sly remark to the guy he was walking with and snigger. The guy looked startled, looked back to check whether Clay had heard, then gave a snigger too.

It comes to this, thought Clay. You hire 'em, feed 'em and cut 'em in on the action, then when they think you're down and on your way out, they turn on you. He nearly flipped, right there outside the depot, but checked himself. He'd show them all, pretty soon. Now was not the time to deplete his little army by even one.

'Hey, you!' he called to the man. The man turned, and Clay felt pleased to see fear in the man's eyes. 'What's your name?' he asked, an edge of contempt in his voice.

'Doone, Lon Doone,' the guy said, thinking, I gone too far this time. Looks like I'm going to have to slap leather here. 'Most folks call me Ace,' he added ingrati-atingly.

'Do they now?' Brunton chuckled, his eyes popping with repressed anger and cold as charity. 'Well, Ace, I got a little job for you, seeing as how you think this whole thing's so humorous.'

'No, I sure don't,' Ace protested, his eyes all the time on Brunton's right hand, which hung low and close to the holstered Colt at his hip. 'It was just that . . .'

'Yup,' Clay interrupted icily, holding up a hand to stem the flow, his left hand, Ace noted. No relief there. He'd heard Brunton was fast, decided if the crazy galoot went for his iron he'd roll to the left, hope to take him by surprise.

'Well, I heard the other day, when I hired you, you were blowing off about being in the army, done some tracking,' Clay said smoothly.

'Sure did,' Ace began eagerly.

'Matter of fact,' Clay continued, 'I remember now that you said that's why they called you Ace, 'count of how good you are at followin' a trail.'

Ace knew he bragged too much, and had a nasty feel-ing his bluff was about to be called.

Clay leaned forward and said quietly, 'Now you go saddle up your horse – the one with the US cavalry brand still on it, Mr Ace Deserter – and you go track that Chinese piece and her beau, John Beamis. I want him dead, and her brought back here, so she can tell me where her cheating, double-dealing buddy Chung Wah is gone, understand?'

'You want me to go alone?' Ace faltered, looking back at the mountain and the wild country beyond.

'Hellfire!' Clay shouted, 'how much artillery do y'want for a little bitty Chink girl and a wounded man? Beamis's most probably dead by now, anyway. Sure ought to be – he left enough blood on the street before that bitch got him on the horse and away. Now, you bring her back.'

'I'll try,' Ace said doubtfully.

'Oh, you do that,' Clay said, 'and if you don't manage it, don't come back, less you want to face me.' He leaned forward, right in Ace's face, and whispered, 'ain't so easy, is it, gettin' a rep? Well, I got one, and if you want to climb up the shitpile and drag me down, boy, you got to get yourself a lot more balls than you have right now. 'Less o'course, you want to go for it right now?'

Ace swallowed. He looked at Clay Brunton, his hand curled snug over his gun butt, his crazy pop eyes glittering with hate, and made a wise decision.

'I'll just go get my hoss,' he said weakly.

Clay turned to the two remaining guys. 'Anyone else want to make any wisecracks?' he asked pleasantly. 'No? Good, now let's go search the town for that chiselling Chinaman. I aim to tear his windpipe out with my bare hands.'

Thirteen

The guy who got nearest to fulfilling Clay's warped little ambition of finding Chung Wah was Whitey Guttridge, though even he wouldn't have placed his chances very high, and would have taken any odds Johnny Beamis laid against it being likely. As bored as all get-out, he wandered down the train from carriage to carriage, chewing on a cheroot and looking indifferently down at the massed Chinese labourers as they huddled in their seats, still cowed by the presence of one of Brunton's gang-members. If Kirk Langley and Chung Wah were on here, he told himself, he would eat his boots. Chung Wah might be hard to spot, amongst all these Chinee, but Langley, well, if he was on this train, then he was the only other white man on it, apart from the conductor. . . . Hey, the conductor!

'Ain't no white men on this train today. Damned heathens put 'em off travelling, I reckon,' the conductor said. He seemed in a bate about something, kept glowering back down the carriages in the direction of his caboose.

'No one in the last carriage?' Whitey asked.

'That's the caboose, and you don't want to go in there, no siree,' said the conductor firmly.

'Why not?'

'Cos that crazy old leper bitch is in there!' the old conductor snapped. 'I put her in the caboose, case any white folk get on further down the line. They sure as hell ain't gonna want to travel with a diseased person. Y'know whose cock's on the block if they report it? Mine, that's whose! I'm gonna get that caboose fumigated when I get back to 'Frisco. You want to get yourself a dose of leprosy, get in there, boy.'

So Whitey steered clear of the end carriage, ambled up and down the rest of the train, looking and looking, and wondering about Brunton's temper when he finally got back and reported his lack of success.

He never did get round to thinking what he'd do if he did come face to face with his quarry. Brunton was not too good in the thinking department, and he picked his men to suit. So it was quite a surprise when Whitey, who had grown a tad confused with walking up and down the train, opened one door too many when he got near to the back, and stepped through, all unannounced, into the caboose.

There sat Chung Wah, dressed up in his Mother Chu robes, with his veil thrown back and the black goggles resting on his forehead like an extra pair of eyes, laughing fit to burst at something the old lady had said. Truth to tell, he was glad to be heading back to 'Frisco, home and dry, with the prospect of making a killing on the gold market once he got back. Wouldn't have been so careless otherwise.

For once Whitey thought fast, and slapped iron into his mitt without pondering. He leant against the wall of the caboose and ranged his pistol over Chung Wah, the old guy and the old woman. All three had been laughing up a storm when he walked in. Now they looked like they'd eaten something they didn't approve of, he thought grimly. Then Whitey wondered just what the hell he was going to do with them all, now that he had them. Hell, why couldn't Brunton have given him some back-up? Only thing to do was wait till the next halt, herd them off at gunpoint and then ride them back to town on the next train.

'OK,' he rasped. 'Just sit pretty and make no moves. That way we all get to live a little longer.'

If Whitey had been the observant type he would have been more prepared for what happened next. Trouble was, he was just too slow and too trusting.

He'd not paid much attention to the little old guy sitting in the last seat of the last carriage as he'd wandered through into the caboose, not given him a second glance. Why should he? He was only another damned Chinese. This one looked peaceable enough, reading a newspaper and making busy little henscratches with a pencil on a notepad.

The little old guy was Ling Weh, ex-swamper at the Magpie Mine, and Chung Wah's business partner. Ling had not paid much attention to Whitey Guttridge either, since he'd found a 'Frisco newspaper on the seat of his carriage when he'd got on, and being as shrewd a businessman as Chung Wah, he'd immediately turned to the stocks and shares page, looked up the section on gold-mines, then checked out what Magpie stocks were running at. Magpie stocks were low, very low, he read. There was even a little article about the mine, and the failure of the owners to find any new veins of ore. The owners, Faulkner and Lewis, had been quite gloomy when asked about future prospects, he read, were rumoured to have started selling some of their own, private, controlling shares. Ling Weh knew well what they were doing: driving the price of shares down, selling some of their own shares at a low price and buying in later, wholesale, when the market had bottomed, to sell out again when the suckers got gold fever. Ling Weh smiled with satisfaction, did some calculations on his pad with his sharp little pencil. When he and Chung Wah got back to 'Frisco they'd make a killing on the market, he thought.

Then he saw Whitey Guttridge walk unsuspectingly past and enter the caboose. Ling Weh waited for Whitey to come running back out once he'd seen the leper nun. When he didn't Ling Weh realized there was trouble. He rose slowly, placed the newspaper on his seat, and, tapping lightly on the door, he stepped through.

It was trouble, for sure. Whitey had a gun in his hand, while Chung Wah, stone-faced, was seated not three yards from the muzzle of it. The old guy with the twisted leg and the old woman were petrified. When they'd agreed to play this pantomime of the leper nun and her escort, back in 'Frisco, they hadn't bargained on getting shot. Fact, they'd been told they'd be shot if they didn't agree.

Whitey was jumpy, the barrel of his gun weaving restlessly between the three Chinese. He was close to losing control, so Ling Weh spoke softly, soothingly to him. Didn't want any silly mistakes right now, when everything had been going so sweetly. 'Message for you, flom Mister Blunton,' at the same time offering the pad slowly toward the gunman from where he stood in the doorway.

'What the. . . ?' Whitey said, unsure. He'd never seen this Chinese before. Who was he?

Ling Weh repeated his message, brought the pad of paper he'd been working prices and profits on toward Whitey.

Whitey fell for it. He kept the gun on Chung Wah and reached out with his left hand for the pad. As he did so Ling Weh dropped the pad, under which he held the pencil like a knife. Swiftly, with a little 'hah!' of expelled breath, Ling Weh brought his arm upwards at an angle, driving the sharp-pointed pencil into the soft piece of flesh behind and slightly below Whitey's left ear. It slid home as if into a sheath. The man made a small, rasping noise in the back of his throat, swayed sideways and was checked in his fall by Ling Weh, who carefully supported Whitey, balanced the corpse's weight back on to its feet, then reached round the body and took the pistol from its right hand. It had all happened very quickly, very quietly; Ling Weh had done it so swiftly that the three other occupants of the caboose were frozen in their positions, as if still under threat from Whitey's gun.

Then, uncoiling from his seat, Chung Wah sprang forward, his yellow nun's habit flying behind him. He took hold of the corpse, pulled the eyelids back to check that Guttridge was dead, then cradled the body in his arms and rotated it so that he could closely inspect the death-wound. He examined the area around the embedded weapon, prodding with his fingers, took hold of the stub end of protruding pencil and tried to withdraw it.

The old man stopped him. 'Better not,' he said. 'It can be messy if you pull it out, and we don't want to leave any signs that he's been in here with us.'

'An amazing piece of artistry,' Chung Wah said. 'You are truly a master.'

The old man now stepped around the corpse and peered behind Whitey's ear, evaluating his work. 'Should have been a sharpened chopstick, really,' he said, gently waggling the inch of pencil that protruded. 'A good-quality ivory chopstick kills them a lot quicker, but this did the job nearly as well, and,' he shrugged regretfully, 'anything at a pinch, as the Americans say.'

Chung Wah could not get over it. He looked and looked, like a kid with his first picture book. He prodded around the wound again, feeling for cartilage and bone. Eventually he looked up in wonder. 'There is absolutely no room for error here,' he marvelled. 'How accurate you were! Tell me something? When you aimed for the spot, did you look at the point of the weapon, or the place you were aiming for?'

'Neither,' the old man said simply. 'I saw the weapon already in place. Now, let's get rid of this body, before someone else blunders in.'

They dragged Whitey's corpse out the back of the caboose, on to the observation platform. Chung Wah made as if to lift and throw it, but the old man stopped him. He waited until the train was running alongside a steep drop, then motioned for Chung Wah to let the corpse fall towards him. He stepped sideways as Whitey slumped towards him, and with a deft grab of the shirt-front and flick of one hip, he launched the corpse into the air. It arced outward, well clear of the rails and went cannoning down the embankment. It crashed down under some pines and rolled out of sight.

Inside the carriage the old woman said to the old man, 'That was vile.' She had her hand pressed to her lips, as if she was going to vomit.

'Careful what you say, wife,' warned the old man. 'These are cold bastards. They are no better than the white men who are seeking us. One word wrong and they would not hesitate to kill us. We don't want to join the *gweh loh*, do we?'

'What a country,' the old woman said, wishing desperately that she could be back home in Canton.

Out on the back platform of the caboose Chung Wah bowed low to Ling Weh. 'I owe you my life,' he said. 'I had no idea that you were an adept in the art.'

Ling inclined his head modestly. 'It's no big deal,' he said. 'I learnt it when I was young. It's always there, once you've learnt the way. Now, pull down your veil and come back inside. There's something in the paper I think will interest you. We're both going to be very, very rich.'

Inside the caboose, Ling Weh held up one hand. 'First I need to walk up the train and see if Brunton sent two men after us,' he said. 'If so, I must dispose of the other. Wait here, Chung Wah.'

'Please,' begged Chung Wah, 'if there is another *gweh loh* after us, send him back here.' He held a chopstick in his hand, taken from his baggage. 'I want to try what you so expertly demonstrated.'

Ling Weh smiled thinly. 'Bet you a hundred dollars you can't hit the spot with the first thrust,' he said, and the old woman turned her head to one side and was copiously sick.

Fourteen

Along with the loss of blood the wound turned septic and Johnny got blood-poisoning. The girl was scared. She barely knew Johnny, but he was all she had to get her back to civilization, and if he died she could be stuck on this mountain for the rest of her life, living with this crazy, hairy man.

Al did his best with Johnny, but he was no nurse, and after the second day he quit and told her the nursing was up to her.

'I've done all I can,' he said to her as she bent over the feverish, unconscious man with a piece of cloth, trying to clean the wound of the badness which seeped from it. 'Guess it's up to you and God now. I'm no nurse, nor no doctor neither.' He laughed bitterly. 'I reckon I'm better at killing men than saving them.' He snatched up his rifle and battered old hat and ran out of the cabin, went down to check his defences, then took off hunting.

For a while she stood and looked at the dying man on the bed, biting her forefinger with fear. She had no experience to tell her what to do, then she thought of the old women in her village when she was a child, of the different cures they had. She remembered the time her mother cut her hand wide open, harvesting rice. Doctors were too expensive, so she had gone to the old women. What had they used?

After a while she left the cabin and, taking an old oak bucket, walked carefully among the plants that Al grew. Finding nothing there, she began to walk back down along the stream that Al had channelled out along the mouth of the canyon to form the defensive swamp. Occasionally she stooped and picked a plant, then discarded it after crushing the leaves and smelling them.

Eventually she found what she was looking for, picked the plants and placed them in the bucket and took them back to the cabin. Some she soaked in vinegar from a cask which she found in the storeroom where Al kept his victuals. Others she crushed and laid directly on the wound. The heat was oppressive in the bedroom, so she brought in all the great earthenware pots which hung from the eaves of the *ramada* with their store of cold spring water inside. She hung these around the bed and as the water inside slowly evaporated they cooled both the room and the feverish man who lay as if dead below them.

Gods, but he stank, she thought to herself, then realized it would be good to bathe him, bring his temperature down and prevent any other infections, so she took a sharp knife, the one Al had used to open the wound so wide as he searched for the slug of lead. She began to cut at the flannel underwear Al had left on Johnny – 'for decency's sake', he had said in a prudish way that had surprised her.

After much cutting and heaving of the heavy body, she had him stripped, and looked at the first naked white body she had seen. Truth be, it was the only man's body she had seen, apart from Chung Wah, who had often made her bathe him and attend on him while he dressed. He had done it, she thought, to remind her of her lowly position as his slave. Though uncle had intended her for Chung Wah's bed, he had not been interested in . . . that from her.

Johnny was even uglier with his clothes off than he was dressed, she decided, so white, and coarse, red hair sprouting here and there, and when she looked down, oh, no, he was so foul looking, so like a horrible beast.

She fetched warm water, soap, a cloth, and as she set to wash his body all over she tried to put her mind elsewhere, to pretend she was not washing a body she was repelled by. Blushing as she reached a part of a man she had never touched before, she made herself think of other things to stop from recoiling. She thought of the old Pearl river, and of Canton. Then she thought that if she even wanted to see 'Frisco again, she had no time for finer feelings or maidenly modesty; she had to make sure the *gweh loh* lived, or she too would most likely die. He was her lifeline. So she grimly washed and soaped, and towelled him dry as tenderly as a mother with her child. When she had done, she applied more poultices from the herbs she'd gathered.

What a life she had had, she thought, going to pick more plants for the evening. First, sold to Chung Wah's uncle, then the humiliation and cruelty she had suffered at Chung's hands, far from home in a strange country, where every man of every colour looked at her in a hungry way, flaunted in their faces by the one man who was allowed to have her, and did not touch her, then thrown away in a card game like a worthless toy. Now, out on a barbarian mountain with a dying man and a crazy who would probably eat her rather than rape her. She asked herself bitterly how she ever got this lucky.

When she got back Johnny still lay like a dead thing,

though the fever was down. She sank down wearily by the bed. So tired, so hot, so dirty. Well, that was soon fixed. Stripping by the bedside, she washed herself all over with luke-warm water from a *cholla*, then dressed herself in a simple cotton undergarment from the small bag she had brought away with her. The cooling strip-bath had refreshed her, and she walked back over to check on Johnny. Just as she leant over him and stroked his forehead absent-mindedly, Al walked in the door and saw Johnny lying there, buck-naked, with his woman, barely dressed herself, every line of her body showing through her durned underwear, looking down at Johnny as if a nekkid man was of no account. Al flamed red, looked away, and then dropped on to the rough table a dozen quail he had trapped.

'I brung these,' he said gruffly. 'Mighty good chow if you make them into a broth for him. Help his belly fight the sickness.'

'Thank you,' she said, wondering what was eating Al now. Then she saw him look at her, then look away, his face red. She looked down at her body, realized how little she was wearing and savvied fast. Al was frightened of women! And she'd been afraid of being left on a mountain with him! She almost laughed with relief.

'I . . . er. . . .' Al shuffled his feet, then snatched up his rifle, opened a box and took out some ammo. 'I figure you might need to be alone, the two of yer, so I got a cave down near the swamp. I'll keep guard there fer a few days, see if that Brunton guy comes after you. If you need anything, just holler – OK?'

'OK,' she said with a smile. Al flinched like she'd pulled a knife on him, and left hurriedly.

She plucked and dressed the little birds and cooked them real slow in a pot. The broth she managed to get down Johnny, but he got a mite messy, since she had to massage his throat to get him to swallow, but at least she got some goodness into him, and began to think that maybe they were over the hump. Then the fever got real bad, so that one minute he'd be sweating rivers, then shaking cold, bone-cold to the touch, and there were not enough blankets to get him warm, not enough in the whole territory. By night time she got into the bed with him and held him tight to warm him.

Eventually she fell asleep and woke towards dawn. He was sleeping, but hot to the touch, burning. She jumped from the bed, and as she fetched cloth and water to cool him, hoped no one would ever learn how she had slept with and hugged such an ugly man, and a *gweh loh* into the bargain. The shame! Being poor, forced into slavery, well, that was just bad luck, the lot of many. But to choose to sleep with a white man, and not even for money, that was revolting to think about. He was of a lesser breed, she truly believed it, and she would be humiliated in the eyes of all her people if it was known what she had done.

Still, as she stripped the sheet back and again began to wash his naked body, she found him less repulsive, even began to admire his body. He was well-muscled from all the shovelling and carrying in his mine, a real worker, this one! She exclaimed when she found the old scar on his leg, puckered and white. That had been a nasty wound, she decided.

It was then that she remembered how her father had been cut once in a fall, not long before he had died, and how her grandmother had carefully collected spiders' webs and placed them over the wound. Grandmother had told her that there was something in the silk the spider made that caused a wound to heal. There was no shortage of webs here, she thought, looking up into the roof space as she dried Beamis's naked body. She climbed on to the table and gathered over a dozen, laying the fragile silks upon her open palm, then climbed down and placed the webs over the oozing wound in Johnny's side, laying them one upon the other with care. Johnny muttered something in his fever and she bent closer to hear. In his delirium he threw one arm around her neck, drew her close to him. She felt something then in the embrace that was close to affection for him, and quickly threw his arm off and looked embarrassedly towards the door, in case Al came back and saw them so close.

Johnny seemed to cool down a while later, and the girl sat by the open door, close to a cooling *cholla* and without knowing it, she drifted off into a light doze. When she awoke twilight was already making the room dark. She quickly looked towards Johnny, saw that he had thrown the sheets off him in his fever, and now was so cold that his teeth were chattering and his body shaking uncontrollably.

How to warm him? There was nothing left to place over him that was warm. Only. . . . She lay on the bed next to him, drew in close and embraced him, felt his naked body against hers, close as a lover's, and held him in her arms, her soft cheek against his harsh, stubbled one. He was the first man she had ever lain with, and she cried silently to herself as night came on. What would happen to her? Would this be the only time she would lie with a man? Once she had had so many dreams.

When she had finished crying she felt him grow even colder, his breath become more shallow and strained. She clasped him oh so tightly, tried to put some of her warmth and life into him. Why should this *gweh loh* have to die? He was a good man, for all he was so ugly. In trying to protect her he had got this wound. Now he would die. She cried then for Johnny, too, as she realized that even though he was of a race she had considered beneath her, he had been far kinder and more humane than her own, for Chung Wah had cast her aside without a second thought, left her to fend for herself rather than take her with him and risk being detected by Brunton and his men. Ki Shing wanted to take her and sell her body to any man with the money. The *gweh loh* had protected her not only from his own people, but hers too. And he had fought to stay on the horse until she was in a safe place, battling the pain and his weakness until she was here.

He was a good man. On an impulse she turned him carefully on his back, stroked his face tenderly, then leant over him and kissed his cold, dry lips. There, she thought, that wasn't so bad; I kissed a *gweh loh,* and I don't feel any different, and she slept then, her arms twined around his naked body.

Fifteen

Clay Brunton was not happy. Reason was he had got his assay report on the samples from the mine he had bought off Chung Wah. The assayer said the mine wasn't worth a plugged nickel. When Brunton had asked how come, since the assay on the first samples he'd brought had pronounced them high quality, the assayer had laughed. Unwisely.

'You didn't say where it come from,' he said. 'You been taken by the oldest trick out. The mine was salted with gold from somewhere else. Look at this.'

He produced some small glass vials with samples of gold ore in them.

'Now this is gold-bearing ore from our side of the mountain, close by the Magpie Mine,' he said. 'Notice the light colour, compared with the samples you took before you bought the mine.'

'So?' Brunton snarled.

'Waal,' the assayer drawled, enjoying the power his knowledge gave him, unaware he was living dangerously. 'Y'see, this gold is from around here, and the other's from way back round the mountain, to the east, I'd say.'

'Not from the Run-Hog-Run?' Brunton asked quietly.

'Nope,' the assayer said firmly. He was a frail, unful-

114

filled sort of guy, and believed that knowledge was power. He was enjoying his moment. 'Fact is,' he said, with a braying whinny of a laugh. 'You been took, partner, by the oldest trick in the book. You been taken for. . . .'

Clay Brunton stepped up right close, bunched the guy's shirt front in his own meaty right hand and brought the stick of a man in real close so that he could smell Clay's cheesy breath and watch those crazy blue eyes pop. By way of emphasis, kinda.

'One word outside of this room,' Clay whispered, his face white with anger, his hand shaking with restrained rage as he held the man, 'and I am going to know you shot your fool mouth off. And I am going to come looking for you. Is that clear?'

'You got it, Mr Brunton,' the assayer gabbled, choking as his shirt front was tightened. 'Silent as a grave, I'll be.' He bit his lip as he realized what he had just said.

Brunton nodded to underline the point, released the assayer and walked to the door of the dingy office. At the door he spun around and looked hard at the man, who was slumped against his desk massaging his neck. He said nothing to him, merely cocked the index and middle finger of his right hand at the assayer's head as if they were the barrel of a gun, his thumb held upright like the hammer of the pistol and his other fingers clenched inward. He closed one eye to aim, depressed his thumb as if he was shooting him.

'Remember,' he whispered, and stepped through the doorway, leaving a very frightened – and quiet – man behind him.

Soon it would be Clay's time to be scared witless, to wonder if everything wasn't slipping out of control, but for a while he stood on the boardwalk outside of his saloon and chewed on a matchstick speculatively. Where

the hell was Chung Wah? Damn near every Chinee had
left town in the two weeks since the fire at the Gam Saan,
and though he and his men had scrutinized the exodus,
he was sure as shit on a shingle that Chung Wah had not
been amongst that frightened stampede out of town. So
where the hell was Chung Wah? Come to that where was
the Chinese whore and Beamis, and Kirk Langley? What
had happened to Whitey Guttridge? Sent him on a damn
train ride, shouldn't have taken more'n a day, and he still
hadn't come back. And what about that fool Ace Doone?
He hadn't shown either, for all his blow about being a
great scout and tracker. He thought deeply on it for a
while. Hell of a lot of people going missing lately. What
Clay didn't know, however, was that one of them was
about to turn up. Right soon.

'Mornin', Clay,' said Dud Johnson, town marshal. A
big, powerful man with a slow way of speaking and a
deceptively mild manner, he moved silently through the
town, and though he sure as hell couldn't stop the killing
in a place where gold dust was the accepted currency and
anything was offered in exchange, he kept it down to an
acceptable level by being frighteningly efficient with fist,
feet and gun.

Clay grunted a reply. He and the marshal were no
friends. They knew too much about each other.

'Take a walk with me, will ya?' Dud asked pleasantly. It
was an order, not a request.

The two walked in silence down Main Street until they
came to Jackson, where Dud bumped Brunton's shoulder with his own, turning him off into the blackened,
burnt-out area that had until recently been Chinatown.

'What the hell is this?' Brunton demanded, coming to
a halt.

'Humour me,' Johnson said, jerking his head towards

the blackened remains of the old Gam Saan, Chung Wah's gambling parlour that had belonged so briefly to Johnny Beamis.

'Got something I reckon you'll be very interested in looking at,' the marshal said over his shoulder as he led Brunton in among the ruins. He seemed to know where he was going amidst all the debris, and as he picked his way toward a board-covered mound he conversed pleasantly to Brunton, a man he loathed.

'You know ol' Mick Hayes, I guess,' he said. Clay only grunted, so he continued, 'Well, day after the fire, when things were cooling down a mite, he came down here and started scratching around. He's a hobo, and knows how to live where another man'd starve. He did quite well, too, on what the Chinese left, after you drove them out.'

'Just what the hell do you mean by that?' Clay demanded, then stopped. Dud Johnson had stopped and was glaring down into Clay's eyes.

'Brunton, you can shit a whole parcel of folk in this town, but please don't try it with me,' he said. 'I'm liable to lose patience, y'hear me?'

Brunton dropped his eyes first, and Johnson nodded to himself, turned and led Clay towards the mound.

'Yep,' he said. 'Ol' Mick found enough to make his scratching around among the ashes worthwhile, but when he got over here, where the gambling place of that Chinese guy was – now what *was* his name? You recall it, Clay?'

'Chung Wah,' Brunton said, through gritted teeth. Hell, he'd a mind to pull a gun now and shoot this bastard in the back. Only his yellow streak stopped him. Even if he did get Johnson, there were some mighty ornery deputies back at the jailhouse who'd take the killing of their boss personally. His son, Matt Johnson, for one. Like his pa, real easy-going, but hell on greased skids when the going got rough.

'Chung Wah – that's the guy,' the marshal said, stopping once more. 'I hear you're looking for him, something to do with a bum mine. Care to tell me?'

'I settle my own disputes,' Brunton snapped, and once more found himself flinching beneath the big man's cold, unwavering gaze.

'Not in my town you don't,' Dud said, 'but we'll talk about that in a while. Now step this way, if you please.'

They came to a halt in front of the mound and a couple of old, fire-charred doors which had been laid over. it. Dud leaned down and made as if to lift one of the doors, then changed his mind, straightened up once more. Despite his anger Clay found his curiosity rising, just as the marshal had intended.

'Anyway,' Johnson continued, 'ol' Mick come over this way, a-scratching and a-digging, till he came on this little mound, all hid away under a pile of burnt-out boards. Well, that got him excited. Thought he'd chanced on the Chinaman's stash, y'know, all the money he'd made at his gambling palace, maybe a huge boxful he couldn't carry out of town and buried for safekeeping. Maybe meant to come back for it later on. Makes sense don't it?'

Brunton grunted once more.

'Care to guess what he found?' Johnson asked. When Clay didn't answer he shrugged and, bending once more, gripped one of the fire-blackened doors and dragged it back.

Clay found himself staring down into a shallow grave, a short trench dug crudely in the sandy, rocky soil. In it lay the corpse of a man whose skin and clothes were lightly crisped, as if roasted in an oven, which, in a way, they had been. The corpse was clearly recognizable as being the last remains of Kirk Langley.

'Friend of yourn, if'n I'm not mistaken,' the marshal said, looking down into the grave. 'You can see that when the fire come it kind of baked him, preserved him well, too. He's been in there at least a couple of weeks now, and he's still as sweet as a nut. Fact, he's a sight more acceptable now than he was when he was alive.' He turned to Brunton and asked, 'Now, what was this dude's name?'

'Langley,' Clay whispered, staring down into Langley's face. 'Kirk Langley. He . . . worked for me.'

Johnson laughed mirthlessly. 'Oh, yeah,' he said, 'a trusted employee. Well, he sure got more than a gold watch when he retired. Someone stabbed him to death. Once in the chest, and once in the throat. You can see from here where the blade went into his throat. Want to see something real interesting?'

Here it comes, Brunton thought. The reason he brought me here. He nodded silently.

The marshal dug in his coat pocket, brought out a used and heat-scorched shotgun shell and plopped it without a word into Brunton's hand. 'Found this and another the same in your man's waistcoat pocket. Notice anything about it?' he asked.

Brunton did, but he shook his head.

'Well, surprised an observant sorta guy like you missed it, but if you look inside the casing you'll see it's got little sparkly bits mixed in with the burnt powder sticking to the sides. Wanna guess what they are?' he queried. Again Brunton seemed lost for words, or unwilling to venture a guess.

'Gold dust,' Dud whispered theatrically, raising a bushy eyebrow. 'Now what's a dead man doing with those on him? I reckon you could tell me quite a bit, Mr Brunton, but since you're going to keep your trap tighter'n a burro's ass in a sandstorm, I'll take me an educated guess, shall I?'

'Guess all you like,' Brunton said sourly, some of his bravado returning. 'You can't pin anything on me.'

The big marshal laughed coldly. 'I don't need to, y'jackass,' he said. 'I am the law in this town. I just need to be pretty sure. Hell, I could kill you without even that, there'd be no one say much about it, but it would trouble my conscience some if I didn't have good reason.'

Brunton didn't know what to say to that. Here was a man telling him point-blank that he didn't like him and he'd as lief kill him as not. Wisely, he decided to keep quiet.

Eventually Johnson broke the silence. 'Hell of a wake, this, ain't it?' he asked. 'Well, you gonna tell me what's been going on here? Why your man died?'

'He ain't my man,' Brunton snapped. 'He . . . just did the odd bit of work for me from time to time.'

'He was your gofer,' Johnson said. 'You shouted shit, and he'd jump on the shovel, so please don't let's pretend different. Wanta know how I see it?'

Again Brunton said nothing, so Johnson continued pleasantly, 'Well, you started lynching the Chinese folk 'bout three month ago, same time as the paper started weighin' in against them. Seemed a patriotic kinda thing to do, huh?'

'You can't prove. . . .' Brunton began, and Johnson closed one eye and smiled lazily. No, he didn't need to. Besides, thought Brunton, he probably could.

'Your man there,' Johnson continued, spitting into the shallow grave, 'helped. Got to be a Saturday night sport. Get some whiskey down their necks for courage, then send your boys into Chinatown looking for an easy mark. String the poor bastard up, then come back to your saloon and talk about what big heroes you all are. You're a bag of shit, Brunton, know that?'

'You can't lay his death at my door,' Brunton snapped, pointing into the grave, at the same time wondering just how the hell Langley had been involved in all this. Had he been in with Chung Wah, and he'd stabbed him to keep his part in the salting of the mine quiet? Or, had he been a partner of Beamis's, and they'd fallen out and Beamis had killed him? It was all getting a mite confusing here.

'Want to know how I see it?' the marshal asked, as if reading Clay's thoughts. When no answer was forthcoming, he began to tell Brunton anyway, talking slowly, piecing it all together.

'Way I see it, you and the paper started in on the Chinee about the same time, aiming to whip folk up, drive 'em out, lock stock and barrel. Why not? It'd worked other places. Beat a few up, harass them on the streets, break a few windows, maybe even lynch one or two. Good sport, huh, Brunton?'

'Don't have a notion what you're talking about,' said Clay, looking down into the cold, sand-filled eyes of Kirk Langley. Anywhere but into Johnson's shrewd face.

Johnson laughed. 'I'll just bet you don't. Question is, did someone put you up to it, or did you just consider it your bounden patriotic duty as a good, solid American citizen, huh?'

'You can't prove nothing,' Clay said, just itching to draw down on this cocky bastard and see him writhing on the floor with a bullet in his ample belly.

'And I already told you, I don't need to, though I wouldn't be too sure about that. You ain't the only guy

who has spies out, y'know. Matter of fact, mine are a hell
of a sight more reliable, since they ain't toadies. They tell
me what I need to hear, not what they think I want to
hear, like yours.'

The marshal scratched his jaw, then went on: 'So, then
little Chung Wah comes on the scene. You've already
been doing some thinking. Why should you just do this
for the fun, or 'cos you just being paid nickels and dimes
for driving out the Chinese? You heard Chung Wah's got
a gold mine, so you tell him you want it – at your price,
naturally. When he won't sell, you kill one or two more
Chinese, leave 'em close to his door, so he sure gets the
message. There's where you went wrong, tangling with
the likes of Chung Wah.'

Something in Johnson's voice made Clay look up
sharply. Johnson cocked an eye.

'Oh, yeah,' he said, 'oh, yeah. You just never guessed,
did you, you dumb prick?'

'I ain't afraid of any John Chinaman,' Clay snapped.
'What are you trying to say?'

'Ever been to 'Frisco?' Johnson asked. 'They got a lot
of Chinese. Cousin of mine works for the police there. I
wired him some time back, right smack after I met
Chung Wah for the first time. I had to go to his place to
take in a white guy who'd wandered in and started shooting into the ceiling 'cos they wouldn't let him play fan-
tan or some such game.'

He paused and stroked his chin, then he said, as if it
genuinely disturbed him, 'There was something about
that Chung Wah, you know? Couldn't put a finger on it,
but he worried me. It was like trying to grab water in your
hand and hold it. One thing I knew for sure, he wasn't
who he was pretending to be. I'd mention his name to
any Chinee in town and they'd clam up tight. A lot of

them seemed real frightened of the guy. I asked around, found he supplied the labour at Faulkner and Lewis's mine, came from 'Frisco. So, I wired my cousin and asked him if he'd ever heard of the guy.'

'And. . . ?' Clay prompted, when Johnson broke off and began building a smoke.

'Oh, he'd heard of him,' Johnson said. 'Seems Chung Wah is not all you took him for, some dumb Chink who fills his pants when a white man barks. Boy, you're stupid, Brunton. How did you ever get this far, huh?'

'Some of us don't scare so easy,' Clay sneered. 'So who is Chung Wah, huh?'

'If you don't know, then I ain't gonna tell ya.' Johnson said smugly. 'Now, where was I? Oh, yeah. So you decide that Chung Wah's gonna give you his mine . . .'

'Hold up there,' Brunton interrupted, going towards his pocket. 'I got . . .'

He was surprised by how quickly the gun appeared in Johnson's hand. And in Brunton's face. For a big guy he moved damned fast, Brunton thought, as he stared into the dark, unwavering little black hole that could belch eternity if Johnson chose.

'Even you wouldn't be such a fool. But I ain't taking any chances,' said the marshal. 'Keep those mitts where I can see them, buddy.'

'I got me a Bill of Sale in this pocket,' Clay said, after he'd swallowed a few times. 'It was all done legal and above board. I paid good money for that mine, and you've no right . . .'

'You're staring down the barrel of the only right I need,' Johnson told him. 'I thought I'd made that clear enough.' When Brunton slowly dropped his hands to his side, the marshal holstered his weapon and continued, 'I know just how much you paid for that mine, and I say

you stole it from the man. Well, no matter. You got took
and you deserved it. Then Chung Wah lost your money
to Johnny Beamis, along with a delectable little slave girl.
Am I right?'

'Who told you?' Brunton whispered.

'I hear things,' Johnson said. 'I'll tell you who didn't
give me the word. Ki Shing.'

'Who?'

'The guy who told you. You remember him, the
Chinee who came looking for you in your saloon? Told
you that Chung Wah was leaving town and had just about
made a present of your cash to Beamis, along with the
girl? Told you that he'd seen Kirk Langley go into the
Gam Saan earlier, as well. So you figured that Langley
and Beamis were in on the scam and went gunning for
both. Know what happened to your snitch, huh? They
found him not long after, outside his brothel with his
head damn nigh cut off. I had to go look at the corpse.
Someone had hit that guy in the neck with a hatchet,
then give him another whack for good measure. No sir,
it sure don't pay to mess with that Chung Wah.'

Brunton's head was whirling. Not for the first time
since he bought that worthless mine off that damned
heathen, he got the feeling that there was a lot happening that he did not know about. One thing, at least he
knew where Kirk Langley was now. But why? Had he
been in on the swindle with Chung Wah and Beamis and
been killed by them, to save splitting the cash three ways?
If so, what use had Langley ever been to them? Brunton
just didn't get it.

'You still don't savvy, do you?' Johnson asked; then as
if talking to a child, slowly and patiently, he said, 'That
day at the mine, Chung Wah shot a snake, right? Well,
the cartridge was full of gold dust and small nuggets.

He'd been there earlier and fired a few off. Maybe he'd been careless or he knew just how stoopid you really are. Whatever, Langley must have picked up a coupla cartridge cases and for once in his life been able to put two and two together and make it come out right. He tried to put the bite on Chung Wah in some way, and Chung Wah killed him.'

Brunton looked at Johnson. Now he began to see the light. Not that it did him any good now.

'Yeah,' the marshal nodded. 'Now you get it, don't you? Shame you weren't so bright back at the mine. Half the town wouldn't have been burnt down, to say nothing of the three white people and ten Chinese killed in a fire I'm damn sure you started. What you gonna do now, genius? Blow the rest of the town up to flush Chung Wah out?'

Brunton glared at Johnson and said, 'I'm going to find that son of a Chinese bitch and kill him, that's what.'

'Haw! Haw!' The marshal's contemptuous guffaw rang out over the wasteland.

'Where is he?' Brunton asked. 'Since you know so damned much, tell me where he is.'

Johnson shrugged. 'No idea,' he admitted. 'I suspect he's left town. My guess is he's back in 'Frisco.'

'The girl and Beamis,' Brunton said with conviction in his voice. 'That's how I'll find Chung Wah. The girl will know where he is. She'll tell me or. . . .'

It was on the tip of Johnson's tongue to tell Brunton to leave well alone, then he decided, what the hell. 'It's my guess that Beamis headed for Lost Canyon,' he told Brunton. Johnson crouched down and sketched a crude map in the dust with his finger. 'Follow the trail out of town, head out over the side of the mountain, so. 'Bout ten, fifteen miles, you'll come to a little stream, follow that up, you'll come to Lost Canyon. The girl and Beamis – if he's still alive – are hiding out there, with a guy named Al.'

'Why're you telling me all this?' Brunton asked suspiciously. 'You don't owe me any favours.'

'Let's just say I prefer any killing that has to be done to happen outside my joorisdiction,' Johnson replied, standing up once more and dusting his hands. He did not make clear who he thought was going to be killed, and Brunton was so stupid, so angry, that he never gave it a second thought. For his part, Johnson forgot to tell Brunton that Beamis, if he was still alive and in Lost Canyon, was hiding out with one of the fastest, most efficient killers the marshal had ever known.

'Besides,' the marshal continued, 'I guess I owe you that much for what comes next.' He threw his coat back so that Brunton could see his holstered Colt and the star on his waistcoat.

'You're finished here, Brunton,' he told the bullying braggart. 'I see you in town this evening, I'm going to kill you. That goes for any of your men, so saddle up, take what you can carry, and don't come back.'

'You ain't got the authority to do that,' Brunton blustered. 'I got friends who'll settle you.'

'You talking about Faulkner and Lewis?' Johnson asked quietly, and watched in satisfaction as Brunton's mouth sagged open in surprise.

'I told you I had spies everywhere,' Dud Johnson said. 'I know you were paid by them to whip up folk against the Chinese and drive them out. Faulkner and Lewis needed to shut their mine down for a month or two, make it look like the whole damn show was going under, no gold left, no labour force. Then they'd buy up all the shares on the market for a morsel of what they were really worth – yeah, bet you didn't know that, either. They play their cards close to their chests, those two. Well, I'll tell you, the secret shift they been running? They found gold, a whole shit-load, I hear. Only it ain't going to do Faulkner and Lewis any good, the crooked bastards. They're finished.'

'How you going to stop them?' sneered Brunton, courage slowly seeping back.

'Oh, I don't need to,' Johnson said. 'They got too clever by half. Put their own controlling shares up for sale while they were still high, figgering to buy 'em back in when they were way, way low. Guess what happened? Somebody in 'Frisco bought every damn share in the Magpie Mine they could lay their hands on, including Faulkner's and Lewis's controlling shares, and now there's a new owner, I hear, controlling the mine through a coupla mining engineers that's come out, a Scotchman called Alasdair McClure, and a German guy by the name of Helmut Benninghoven. Met 'em today, when I was down at the station, seeing Faulkner and Lewis off. Nice guys.' Johnson stroked his jaw and grinned evilly at Brunton. 'Know who I reckon is the new owner of the Magpie?'

'Chung Wah!' Brunton said with a blinding flash of insight.

'Well, hell! Y' finally got there!' Johnson said. He turned and spat into Langley's grave, then said, 'If you come back here, I'll lay you alongside of your buddy, Brunton. Looks kinda happy, don't he? Guess the roasting he got is nothing to the temperature where he's gone. He'll be waiting for you, remember, if you come back.'

Brunton took one last look into Kirk Langley's scorched and frightening visage, then turned on his

heel, to round up what few of his men remained. In his
heart was hatred for Chung Wah, who thought himself so
clever. Well, he'd dance to Brunton's tune once he had
found the girl and she'd told him where to find the chiselling Chinese bastard. Behind him he heard Dud
Johnson scraping sand and rocks back into Langley's
grave with his heavy boots. Whistling while he did it, too.

Sixteen

It was five days before Johnny came to. He heard quail calling and hens clucking and fussing outside, and for a moment thought he was a child again in bed. Then he realized that someone was pressed against his back, their warmth keeping him warm. He felt soft breath on his neck and the wonderful silkiness of a woman's thigh, belly and breasts against his naked back. One arm lay gently over his, the small hand on his chest. Who was it? He opened his eyes and saw the rough adobe walls of Al's hideout, tried to turn in the bed and see just who she was, this mystery woman who had cradled him in her sleep through the night. But as he turned his wound stabbed pain through his side, and he groaned out loud.

The girl awoke swiftly and leapt from the bed. Johnny turned now, more slowly, to face her where she stood by the bed, her hands crossed over her breasts, wearing only a thin silk shift. Sunlight streaming through the door shone through her flimsy nightwear and left little to Johnny's imagination.

'At last, you awake,' she said, her face flushed with embarrassment. 'Feel OK?'

'Weak,' Johnny said, 'but I think I'll live. We at Al's?'

'Yes. You got us here. I thank you,' she said.

'Hey, I guess I should thank you,' Johnny said. 'Outside Chung Wah's place – how long ago?' He whistled when she told him six days, then said, 'You shot that guy, saved my life. Then you got me here. Who nursed me – you and Al?'

'Al got bullet out,' she said. 'I nurse you.'

'So I owe you my life twice over,' he said flatly.

'Back in town,' she said, 'it would have been easy to sell me to Ki Shing, or let Brunton take me. Either way I finished if you not protect me. Why you bother? You get into all this trouble, nearly killed, because of me. No, I thank you, Johnny Beamis.'

Johnny laughed, or tried to. God, that hurt.

'Well, I guess that makes us quits,' he said. 'Where's Al?'

The girl giggled. 'He living in cave down by swamp,' she said. 'Women make him nervous!'

Ain't surprised she spooked Al, if that's all she's been wearing, Johnny thought, then looked at her, really looked at her for the first time since she had stepped out of the darkness in the Gam Saan and been given to him as his prize for turning up an ace against Chung Wah's king.

Some pot, he thought now, as he looked at her. She was not too slender – he hated skinny women – but with a good figure, strong thighs, and breasts not too large, he guessed, by the way she had her arms almost flat across her chest. Her face was what captivated and intrigued him, though, so unusual was it to Johnny, who was used to the idea of fair white skin, round faces, round eyes. Her skin was the colour of faded linen, almost ivory, and her eyes, black as obsidian, almond-shaped, flashed and glowed deep beneath delicate eyebrows. Her cheekbones were high and prominent, and her small nose almost flat to her face. She caught him staring at her, blushed again and turned as Johnny coloured up too and looked away.

'Turn your back,' she said. 'I will dress.'

Johnny turned and as she dressed in the trousers and jacket she'd worn when they had ridden away from the Gam Saan she filled him in on how they had gotten here, on his fever and how Al thought Johnny would die. She talked of the different plants she had found to make the poultice, of the spider webs and how she figured they had drawn the badness from his wound and helped it heal. She was aware that she was prattling on, but she was discomfited that he had awoken to find her almost naked, wrapped around him.

'Glad you didn't give up on me,' Johnny said, aware of her reason for talking on and on.

'That is why, this morning, you know,' she said, her speech broken with embarrassment. 'Because of the fever, I sleep in the bed, keep you warm.'

A smart remark sprang to mind, like, call back soon, but Johnny did not give it. This woman was different. And he owed her his life.

There was a cough from the doorway. Al stood there. He wore a sand-coloured poncho and long baggy leggings. On his head was a shapeless hat, also sand coloured. In his arms he cradled a rifle.

'Hey, you're awake,' he said, and grinned at Johnny. They were old buddies, ever since Johnny, in his tender-foot days of prospecting, had come across Al with a bust ankle and brought him back on his mule, the unex-ploded Number Nine, to Lost Canyon and safety, which was the only reason why he was here now. Al trusted few callers. The rest ended up dead.

'What the hell you wearing?' Johnny asked Al.

'Blends with my surroundings,' Al said. 'The poncho breaks up the lines of my shape. Often dress like this when I'm watching for visitors. Speakin' of which, you expectin' anyone to come looking for you and your lady here?'

Johnny and the girl looked at each other. Just for a moment they had thought they were free and away. But they both knew Brunton. Of course he would send someone after them.

'Guess so,' Beamis sighed. 'You spotted someone?'

'Not sure yet,' Al said, 'but I think there's somebody snooping around. Come see for yourself.'

Johnny tried to get out of bed, but his legs gave way, and he fell back, sweating suddenly, his wound giving him hell. The girl pushed him back under the blankets and propped him up.

'You stay,' she said. 'If it Brunton I come tell you.'

'Listen,' Johnny said, 'if there is someone, don't take any risks, huh, Al?'

'Don't worry,' said Al. 'They's no way anyone can get in here without a battle.' He ducked out the low doorway and the girl followed him, after giving a brief, reassuring smile to Johnny, who'd never felt so damn useless in his life.

Outside Al led the way through the brittle bush and ocotillo until he and the girl reached a clump of paloverde by some rocks at one side of the canyon's mouth. Here he helped her climb up until they were lying on an upsloping rock, shielded by bushes, looking back along the trail they had followed to get here. She thought to herself that it seemed so long ago; though it was less than a week, she was convinced that she would be killed or, even worse, caught by Brunton. Her only hope a dying *gweh loh.*

The trail as it snaked around the shoulder of the mountain before dipping down to the plain and the swampy mouth of Lost Canyon was masked in places by rocks and trees, and she could see nothing moving in the vast spread before her.

'Where?' she asked, looking out over miles of empty, quiet country.

'Over yon,' Al said, jerking his head forward towards the trail. 'There's something up there that's just a-sitting, looking down here, waiting to see if it's safe to come down.'

'How you know?' she asked.

' 'Cos I've been sitting here, looking back since morning light,' Al said, and the girl thought, what a way to live, so frightened that someone was going to come in and take your life that you spend most of it worrying and watching, existing, not living.

'How many men?' she asked.

'Doesn't have to be a man – or men,' Al said, squinting his eyes as he scanned the area. 'Could be cougar, but I don't think so. Would have moved on by now. Maybe Injuns, but I doubt it. They been finished off for the last few years round these parts, on reservations an' such. Guess you'd know about that, miss.'

'Why?'

'Well, you bein' Indian yourself. What tribe are ye?' Al asked. 'Apache, Comanche?'

The girl stifled a laugh. 'I'm Chinese,' she said.

'Well, hell,' said Al, scratching his great, wild beard and looking hard at her. 'You the first I ever seen. Chinee, eh? You could pass for Indian, y'know.'

'*Gweh loh* kill Indians too,' the girl said bitterly. She nodded upward. 'How you sure someone up there?' she asked.

'OK,' Al said, reaching under his poncho and producing a spyglass. He pointed towards two distant specks in the sky, growing larger by the second. 'They's a pair of black-necked stilts, flying in to drink at the swamp,' he said, adjusting his glass and looking up the mountain through it. 'Going to fly right over our caller. Watch 'em through this.'

He handed the spyglass to her, cautioned her not to lean forward out of the shade of the bushes they were under or the lens would catch the sun, alert any observer up there on the mountain to their presence.

The girl watched as the birds rapidly neared the spot Al had pointed out, their long legs clearly visible tucked beneath their bodies. As they came in lower and neared the bushes and rocks at the turn of the thin trail she saw them suddenly veer away, making a wide detour before they checked in their flight and lazily descended over the swamp, splashing down among the reeds.

'Thought so,' Al said. 'Can't see birds that high up letting a cougar or such spook them. Now we got us a problem. There's at least one guy up there looking down at us, and we're down here looking back up. One side has to make the first move.'

'What they do if we just wait?' she asked.

'Well, they're looking for someone. I guess it's you two,' Al said, stroking his jaw. 'If it was me up there, I'd come down at night-time and have a snoop round, maybe hole up where I could get a good line of fire into the canyon come morning. 'Course, that ain't too easy, since I put up all these defences, like the swamp and the tripwires.'

The girl scrutinized the mountain through the spyglass.

'What's to stop watcher climbing above us, coming in from top of end of canyon?' she asked.

'Look hard,' Al said. 'Whole mountain from there on in is shale on the surface. The mountain cap is a softer rock, and it's wearing down. It's on the move all the time. Old Indian name for this place is Shivering Mountain. That's why the trail comes down just there. Ain't safe any further, not even for mountain goats. And that's why whoever's up there is sticking. They know they got to leave their hiding place sooner or later, either come down that trail or back off and find another way into the canyon for a good look round. But they know that if they back off that might give you time to get away, if you are holed up in here. 'Course, it could be they're playing a waiting game, hanging fire till reinforcements are within sound of signal-shots. Y'know, fire off a pistol, bring the whole pack running to us.'

'I don't understand,' the girl said, lowering the spyglass and looking at Al. 'You say you kill plenty men come here?'

'Yeah,' Al said grimly. 'There's quite a few buried around here.'

'Why you not just kill this one? What you worry for?'

Al scratched his beard. 'Well, for a start, we don't know there's just one of them up there. There could be a whole bunch. Now, I'm fast, but if they spread out, they'll get me. Y'see, miss, these defences are OK so long as they's just the one man, and usually they only come in ones to get me.'

'Why?' the girl asked a question she had pondered on ever since she had arrived here.

'A long time ago, and in a place a long way away, I earned myself quite a rep,' Al said. 'Y'know what I'm talking about?'

'And these men that come, they want to steal your rep from you?' she wanted to know. She looked around, to see if she could see this strange object, the rep which Al spoke of.

Al laughed. 'You could say that,' he said. He explained then what was meant by having a reputation, how a man's fame spread, lies were told, and even when they weren't believed, other men wanted to kill you, purely for the fame of having killed the man the stories were told about. He told her how with age his desire to kill – and his speed – had passed.

'Left me with the same low cunning that made me so good,' he told her, 'and I'm still a sight faster than your average Joe, but hell, I just ain't got the belly for it any more. So, over twenty year ago I come out here.'

'And men come here to kill you, still?' she asked, incredulous.

Al shook his head in sorrow, as if he found it hard to believe too. 'Yep,' he said. 'Somehow, somewhere they hear some fool telling the story, that there's an old crazy guy living out in the back of beyond who folks reckon is . . . well, it don't matter what my name was. It ain't that now, but if you stay in this country long, you'll hear it.' He lifted his head, said proudly, 'I used to be famous. Even back East they knew my name. They wrote books about me. I seen one once, got a travellin' salesman to read me a piece of it. Lands, it was a parcel of lies! Anyways, how it all works is, some kid who's half-way decent with a gun hears the story about me hiding out here, says no, that guy's been dead years. And then someone says, oh yeah, did y'ever hear who killed him, where, why, when? Then the kid gets to thinking maybe I really am out here, and he comes to see who's fastest, me or him. So far, it's allus been me. Then I've killed another man, taken another life, just so I can go on living this miserable half-life, hiding out in the wilds like a savage animal.'

'Maybe people forget one day,' she said gently.

Al laughed bitterly. 'And maybe not,' he said. 'In any case, how do I find out? Ride into a town somewhere and see how long it takes before I'm recognized and gunned down? Know how long I'd last if I did that now? About a day, tops, I reckon. Territory I did my killing in, I'd last ten minutes at the most. I'm a trophy, missy, like some deer with a good rack of antlers.' He shifted uneasily on the rock and looked again up the mountain. 'Now how in hell are we going to get that jasper out of his hide up there?' he mused aloud.

'Stay hidden. I show you,' said the girl, and sliding back off the rock she walked out into the open. Unbuttoning her shirt as she went, she walked down towards the stream where it flowed into the swamp, in full view of whoever or whatever was up there, watching the canyon.

Seventeen

Thing was, Ace Doone was no ace, but he wasn't completely hopeless as a tracker, and when Brunton kicked him out and told him not to come back 'less he found where Beamis and the girl were hiding out, he set to with a will, determined to show the ignorant, crazy bastard that by God he could do it!

Not that he had too hard a job. Beamis had bled like a stuck pig for a while, and left a trail of gory splashes to follow for quite a ways, and with two riders on its back the old nag's hooves had dug deep where the going was soft. So, after a couple of days of careful tracking, sometimes having to cast back miles in the broken country, getting lost up box canyons and down dry arroyos, Doone had got close to the pair of fugitives. Then he lost it all through being too confident, got discouraged and took a day or two out, and when he had finally decided the hell with it all he came across another couple of dried blood-splotches on a rock, picked up the distinctive hoof-marks further on and set off again.

So, by luck and skill, he came at last to a point over-looking Lost Canyon. The hoof-marks he'd tracked led down on to the plain there and headed towards the canyon and it looked a definite possibility. Might be worth a looksee.

Whether it was because he was an old army man or whether there was just something so quiet, so watchful, about the canyon, Ace could not say, but he spent a cold night up on the trail, under the bushes and rocks, his horse tethered nearby, watching and waiting to see if someone was watching and waiting also, just aching to drygulch him. Just a few hours, a day maybe, he told himself. Time was on his side. Beamis was wounded, probably dead, and the girl didn't know her way around. She did know the way to that Chung Wah, though, who'd got Brunton so good and riled, and that should be worth ready money when Ace found her and brought her back. So, softlee, softlee, catchee monkee, as the Chinese say. He lay low and watched the canyon. Give it till noon, he thought, then I'll have to work out a way of getting in there, take a look round. Maybe wait till night, go in by moonlight.

He was still debating which was best when he saw the girl below, large as life and a hell of a sight lovelier. She walked towards the stream, stripping off her shirt as she came, then knelt and washed herself thoroughly in the cold water. 'Course, it was too far to see anything, but Ace had a wild imagination, and he began to wonder if maybe he couldn't just cut a piece of the action here for himself. There was no doubt about it being the girl, he thought, with her long, black hair and skin colour. 'Less, of course, it was an Indian. Nah, he thought, ain't no such animal, not in these parts no more. Which was why he'd deserted and made for these parts.

What was she doing now? Engrossed, he peered out from under his bush, still careful not to stick his head out too far. Hell, she'd dried herself on her shirt and had put it back on. Damn! Hey! She was crying, looked like it anyway, sitting all scroodled up, clutching her knees and now and then lifting up her head and holding her hands to her face. Even from this distance, Ace could see her shoulders shaking, and in the clear mountain air her sobs and wails carried: 'Oh, Johnny, Johnny! What I do now?'

That settled it. Beamis was dead. She was alone. Ace nearly bust out laughing. It was all so easy. All he had to do now was go down there and take her. For a moment he thought of going to fetch his horse, just in case she decided to make a run for it when she saw him. Then he thought, where's she gonna run to? Nah, he'd walk down there and grab her now, while she was still wailing. Time to think about getting back to town when he had the bird in the hand. Slowly he got up, eased his cramped joints, then set off down the mountain trail, walking as quietly as possible, his rifle held on the girl in case she tried anything.

Through her long hair which hung down over her face she saw him approaching and renewed her wailing. She was frightened, but calmed herself. She had no plan. Maybe Al would shoot the man, but he'd seemed a little wary of loosing off a shot, in case there were others nearby. Well, she'd wait and see what this *gweh loh* did when he got to her. She heard him splashing through the swamp as he gave up all pretence now of stealth, risked another peek and saw him standing above her.

'Hey, girl, where's Johnny Beamis at, huh?'

She looked up into his cruel face. A brighter man than Ace would have noticed that despite all the wailing and crying there were no tears on her cheeks.

'Johnny, he dead. Blunton's men shoot him an' he die,' she said, sniffling. 'He up in canyon. You come see, help bury him?'

'Nah,' Ace said. 'Leave him for the buzzards. We got some riding to do. Brunton wants to talk to you, little lady.'

At mention of Brunton's name the girl began wailing again. 'Please, please, no takee me to Blunton. He bad man, hurt this little Chinee girl,' she said.

Ace was also beginning to think that it was maybe a bad idea. What would Brunton give him for her, anyway? Why not take what he'd got and head for pastures new? She could amuse him for a while, then, well, he'd just sell her on. That Chinese brothel owner, the one who'd come sneaking in that night to tell Brunton about the scam Chung Wah had pulled on him had offered to buy her off Brunton when he had finished with her. Others would pay good money, too, when Ace had had enough of her. She was a looker, no doubt about it. He leant down to pull her up by her hair, give her a light smacking, show her who was boss. But she grovelled at his feet, began clasping his boots and begging him not to take her back.

If Ace had had a grain of sense he would have cast his mind back not so long ago to the night when Brunton went steaming in to the Gam Saan and tried to take the girl from Beamis. Ace had been told – warning enough for any guy with savvy – that the girl had thrown a man heavier than him clear across a room when he'd laid hold of her. Bust his wrist and dislocated his shoulder for good measure. Like most of the heavies employed by Brunton, however, Ace was not a great thinker. How could it be otherwise? Guys with the smarts stayed away from Brunton. Guys like Doone ended up doing his dirty work.

So when the girl gripped his lower legs, wrapping her arms tight round them whilst snivelling on his boots, Ace was well pleased. The relationship seemed to be getting off to a good start.

He was less than pleased when she suddenly wrenched his feet upwards into her chest whilst blocking his forward impetus with her left shoulder. Ace had time to let out only a rather weak and unmasterly 'Hey!' before he was dumped with no vestige of masculine superiority on his ass. The back of his head hit the ground and he was dazed for a moment. Before Ace could gather what few wits he had he'd been flipped over to lie face down. The girl sat astride him holding in her other hand a long, slim knife which she had last used for preparing quail and which she now pressed firmly to Ace's neck.

'No move, or you dead asshole,' she warned him. Chung Wah would have criticized her English, but approved of a move he had taught her. There'd been a shortage of sparring partners back in town. He'd had to practise his *kung-fu* in secret and had taught his slave-girl much. Ace lay still and wondered what to do now. He didn't have long to wait. He heard boots approaching, felt his gun being lifted from its holster.

'OK, missee, ease up on him now. You, feller, roll over and face me,' came the voice.

Ace did as he was told, found himself looking up at some old galoot whose unshaven face put him in mind of an exploded mattress. He didn't look at the old-timer for long, however. What really caught his attention was the rifle, about three feet from his face, far enough for him not to grab at it, close enough to do some major exploratory work of his brain pan if the trigger got pulled.

'Nope, don't recognize you,' Al said. 'So you'll be...?'

'Doone, Ace Doone,' came the gabbled reply. 'Listen, I didn't mean no harm to the girl here, mister ... I didn't catch yer name?'

'Didn't throw it,' Al said. 'Back on your face, pronto!' Ace did as he was told – fast. Al got him to roll over and stick his face down in the dust, then said, 'An' you'll be working for that bag o' slime, Clay Brunton?'

'No, never heard of him,' said Ace, his voice just a tiny bit muffled on account of the soil he was talking into. 'I'm just passing through.'

'Now, I hear well,' Al said pleasantly, and he prodded the rifle's barrel-end into Ace's neck a shade harder. 'And I heard you mention Johnny Beamis, and Clay Brunton. Ain't that a poser for us both?'

'Both?' Ace mumbled. God, but he was itching to turn over and look into the old fart's eyes, see what he could guess about his intentions.

'Yeah,' Al answered. 'For me, 'cos I have to decide if you lying to me, and for you, 'cos if you are, I shoot you.'

Ace's shoulders slumped. Time to snow the old loon. He put on his most earnest face, not that it was much use to either him or Al, buried deep in soil.

'OK, mister,' he admitted. 'I'll level with you. Brunton did send me after the girl and Beamis. He's spitting angry, wants to get hold of a guy called Chung Wah. Figgers the girl here knows where she is. But I had enough of him. I really was passing through when I chanced upon the canyon here. I saw the girl and come down to talk. Honest.'

For a while Al seemed to ponder, then he nodded slowly, as if accepting Ace's story. Then he jerked his head up towards the hideout on the trail, where Ace had been spying on them for so long.

'Go get his horse, if you can find it,' he told the girl,

and with a scowl at Ace's prostrate form, she did as she was bidden.

Once she was gone Al really began to work on Ace. He kicked him in the ribs a time or two, just to make a point, then said:

'OK. That's fine. The girl's gone – allus hate to kill a man in front of womenfolk.' He sashayed the magazine of the rifle back and forth loudly, then pressed the muzzle hard back in the nape of Ace's neck once more.

'For God's sake, mister,' Ace pleaded, sobbing by now. 'Don't kill me. I'll do anything you ask.'

'Nah,' Al said, as if considering it. 'I've been through this kinda crap before. 'Sure, you'll swear to anything right now. But you won't keep your word.'

The conversation sawed back and forward for a while, Ace assuring Al that he was basically an honest guy and would keep a deal, Al telling him he'd rather not make a deal; it was less fuss to kill Ace now, where he lay. Eventually Al got Ace so scared he told him everything he knew about Brunton and his gripe with Chung Wah, even down to the stupid aside Ace had passed at the rail depot which had got Brunton so riled and caused Ace to be sent out here.

'Well, we'll be seeing that sack o' shit Brunton soon, I guess,' Al said, and, soft as axle grease, Ace replied, 'No sir, he's a-waiting on me to report back in town as to where Beamis got to.'

Even as Ace said it, he bit his tongue and silently repeated, all unknowing, Kirk Langley's last words, 'Oh, shit!' Ace was that little bit brighter than Langley; he realized he'd just told the old crazy that he had come out here alone, that any shot would go unheard, would not bring anyone else moseying over to see what was happening. In short, it was safe for Al to kill him.

Definitely an 'Oh shit' situation.

'Mister,' Ace quavered. 'Please don't shoot me.'

Al was in a bind. Most guys who came looking for him he shot face to face, let them take the draw, or he shot them from a distance, clean and quick. This would be quick, but to shoot an unarmed man, lying down, in the back of the neck, was difficult. Difficult, but not impossible. He took a breath, steeled himself, then heard the sound of the girl, riding Ace's horse in, its hoofs splashing as it came through the swamp. Damn!

She reined in by the side of the two men and scrambled down. Her look towards Al was enough. She could tell what was going through his mind, and as he glanced at her, she shook her head and looked pleadingly at him. OK for her, he thought sourly. It's my skin too, and in a week or so, Beamis'll be fit to travel, and they'll be gone. Ain't nowhere for me to go.

Ace continued to blub and plead. He told them he wouldn't go back to town, honest, he'd just keep riding. He'd forget everything he'd seen here, he'd tell no one. He snivelled and moaned till Al pulled the rifle out of Ace's neck, ordered him to his feet and shoved him roughly with the barrel of the rifle towards his horse.

'Get riding,' he ordered, 'and head west, on yon trail. When you reach the leaning rock over there, don't loop east toward town. Just keep riding, forget about Beamis and her, and particularly about me, if you want to stay in good shape. Got that?'

Ace got it, he swore he'd got it. He gabbled out his thanks and fair swarmed aboard the horse. He spurred it up and was away without a backward glance.

The girl came to stand beside Al, and made as if to speak, but he hushed her, brought up his rifle and beaded it on Ace's back.

'What you do?' the girl asked in alarm. 'You promise you not shoot!'

'He also promised to head west and forget about me,' Al said, squinting down the sights. 'But he's a wiseass, and pretty soon he's gonna forget his promise and remember how small you and me made him look, and he's gonna figger we was just lucky, got the drop on him. Then, when he figgers he's outa range. . . .'

Just before Ace reached the leaning rock, Al grunted and said to the girl, 'See? His shoulders have come back.' The girl gave him a puzzled look, and Al explained, 'Means he's feeling safe, probably reached some sort of decision. When your life depends on it you watch men, learn to tell by how they carry themselves what they thinking, what they gonna do.'

Sure enough, at a distance of just over six hundred yards, Ace turned his horse and looked back on the couple, standing at the edge of the swamp, small in the distance. He'd been measuring off the gap between himself and safety by his horse's strides, at first thinking that Al might change his mind and shoot him in the back, but when Ace got up to nigh on six hundred yards, he realized he was safe. No one could shoot and kill over such a distance with such a dinky little rifle like the crazy guy was carrying, Ace told himself, and with the glow of safety came a slow anger that built up as he dwelt on how the old galoot and that Chinese whore had humiliated him. Ace wanted revenge, and how. And he wanted them to know – and be afraid.

'Hey, Methuselah!' He yelled, his voice still hoarse from all his begging and sobbing. 'Y'think I ain't gonna get you for this? Think I'm just gonna ride out and not let Brunton know?' Then another realization struck the tracker, a glorious revelation that had been at the back of his mind since he first saw Al, born of idle talk around camp-fires from men who knew the country and the characters for fifty years past or more, who told the old legends of injun fighters and gunmen and outlaws and. . . .

'Hey!' he crowed, standing as high as he could in the stirrups so his voice would carry to the man. 'I know who you are! I heard about you! Well, you can kiss my . . .'

'Crack!' the thin noise of the rifle's explosion had barely time to begin to echo up and down the canyon, to bring Johnny Beamis leaping quickly and painfully from his bed, before Ace had pitched sideways from his horse and crashed into a clump of manzanita.

The dinky little rifle Al had been carrying was a Whitworth, an English gun used during the war by Confederate snipers. Though it was only a .45 calibre it was awesomely effective at up to a mile in the hands of a man who knew how to use it. It was Ace Doone's pure bad luck that he decided to sass a guy from six hundred yards who did know. The manzanita moved wildly for a few seconds as Ace threshed around, then was still.

'He dead?' the girl asked.

'Sure is,' Al replied after watching the manzanita for a while.

'What we do now?'

'Waal, we better clear away pronto, get his horse out of sight and bury him, 'case there is anyone following. Turkey vultures are one hell of an easy marker to spot. I'll go get the horse and watch for anybody sniffing round. Can you get a shovel from the store room, miss. Know what a shovel is?'

The girl looked at him for a while, then began to laugh strangely. 'Oh, yeah, I know what shovel is,' she said. 'It for cleaning up horse shit and burying dead *gweh loh.*' She turned away and headed for the canyon, still laughing to herself.

'Right,' Al said uneasily. Whatever. Took folks different ways, he guessed. She sure was a cool one, though. First she wanted the guy spared. When he drops the dude, she's laughing her tits off. Women. He'd never understood them, never would.

Johnny met the girl half-way. He'd managed to find his Colt when she and Al had left, and he'd lain on the bed for a tense half-hour, listening out for their return, worrying himself sick and computing the odds of getting out alive if it was Brunton out there. When the rifle went off, he'd eased himself painfully from the bed and hobbled his way down in the direction of the gunfire, frightened that the girl had been shot.

'You OK?' he asked her, seeing tears in her eyes and on her cheeks.

She brushed her tears away. 'I OK,' she said wearily. She turned and pointed to Al, out beyond the canyon, walking towards where Ace's body lay. 'Just another man killed, is all. We bury him, everything OK.'

'Who . . .' Johnny began, but his words were cut short by a salvo of rifle fire, and even as he grabbed the girl and pulled her unceremoniously to the floor the bullets came winging in, kicking up little spurts of dust around them. Together they crawled to the scant shelter of a few rocks, where sporadic fire pinned them down.

From his hiding place Johnny saw Al turn, jump aboard Ace's horse and gallop furiously towards the refuge of the canyon, rifle in hand. He hadn't a chance; the new arrivals were well sheltered in the bushes and rocks that half an hour before had hidden Ace Doone from view. A shot took Al from his horse, leaving him lying in full view of his assailants. Without thinking,

Johnny leapt to his feet and began to run awkwardly over the open ground to rescue Al, thinking, even as he made his painful way, his side hurting like hell, that these were not good odds for a gambling man to take on. Strangely, the fire stopped as soon as he hove into view, and he fell to the floor at Al's side unhurt.

Then from the heights came a voice that both Beamis and the girl recognized, only now it was gloating, cock-sure.

'Hey, Beamis, y'hear me? Speak or we fire, and we sure got you in our sights, boy!' As if to encourage him a few bullets came winging his way, and both Beamis and Al crouched as low as they could, pinned down by the fire.

'Who the hell is it?' Al hissed, 'Brunton?' When Beamis nodded ruefully, he cursed and said, 'There's two or three others with him, judging by the lead that's flyin'. Damn me for a fool, getting caught out here!' He spat in the direction of the nearby corpse of Ace Doone. 'And damn him fer lying to me,' he said savagely. 'Now what the hell do we do?'

Eighteen

Ace hadn't been lying when he told Al that he was on his own and Brunton was still in town. As ever, though, he'd not really known the score. He wasn't to know that Brunton had been kicked out of town and was on his way to Lost Canyon, courtesy of Dud Johnson, who'd handily pointed out the way, figuring that Brunton needed killing if only to do the world a favour.

Six guys had ridden out of town, but within hours three had split from Brunton's little posse. Andy Hacket had been the first, when he'd heard just where they were heading.

'Whoah,' he said, reining in and pulling at his hatbrim thoughtfully, 'then count me out of that one. I heard things about that place. And the old guy who lives there. No sir.'

Brunton had argued and threatened, but Hacket had turned his horse's head and made off, saying, 'Folks go in there, they don't come back. Why in tarnation do you think Johnson pointed you in that direction?'

'Durn coward,' Brunton had fumed, but the others knew Hacket well. He was a game one, not afraid of a fight, either fist or gun. If he declined the odds, well, there must be something in it. When Brunton wasn't

150

watching, Court Rhodes angled his roan away, with Al Stevens following, both keeping their hands close to their guns and their eyes on Brunton's back; they guessed they'd try their luck in Texas. So it was that Brunton came to Lost Canyon with only the two biggest deadbeats he'd ever set on in tow, Mac Rawlins and Bob Deyton. They came because they didn't have the savvy to think for themselves and they weren't much use on their own.

Brunton had been a week behind Ace Doone, but with Johnson's boot up his rear and a pointer on where to look for Beamis he didn't meander like Ace, and when the party heard the crack of the rifle that signalled Ace's death they were within a mile of Lost Canyon. Spurring their horses, they were in time to see the Chinese girl heading off up the canyon and Al walking out to a guy lying dead by a horse Bob Deyton swore was Ace Doone's. Didn't take a genius to work out what had just happened, which was a mercy, given the collective brain-power present. Strategy was just as simple.

'Shoot the bastard,' Brunton ordered. 'Then we'll ride in and pick up the girl.'

It came as a surprise when Beamis came hobbling across to Al's rescue too, but by then Brunton was grinning broadly. Things were going his way again. A little more time, and he'd have Beamis and the girl and from one or both of them he'd learn the whereabouts of Chung Wah.

He spat and thought, 'So much for Chung Wah hiding out in 'Frisco! He never got that far. Bet he's hiding out around here. Well, they'll soon tell me, and I'll get to stretch the swine's yellow hide across a rock.'

'OK, Beamis,' Brunton yelled. 'You got one chance to save yourself. Stand up slow, hands in the air, the guy

with you too. Get up, or we'll shoot you where you lie.'
To emphasize his point he sent a few shots thunking into
the ground around them.

'Getting close,' Al said. He had been hit in the right
arm, a glancing blow that had laid the flesh open.
Stoically, he bore with the pain and began scheming on
how to get out of this one without incurring any more
injury. He slid his sidearm from its holster with his good
left hand and stashed it in the back of his pants.

'Guess we got no choice right now but to stand,' he
said to Johnny, grunting with the pain from his shoulder.
'You still got that Colt with you? Good, tuck it in your belt
behind you, like I got mine. What we do, if things get
rough, we try and make it back to the canyon, firing as
we go. OK? Run in zig-zags to make a harder target for
'em.'

'What about your rifle?' Beamis asked, indicating the
Whitworth lying at their feet.

'Leave it lie,' Al answered regretfully. 'We're both
wounded, and you can't run. You'll be slowed down even
more with a rifle, and you can't fire accurate without
standing still and making a good target for that scum up
there. We just aiming to keep their heads down much as
we can. You ready?'

Beamis nodded, and slowly they rose to their feet,
automatically crouching, their hands raised.

'OK,' shouted Brunton. 'Now call the girl out, and tell
her to come out with her hands clean. I see that damn
shotgun she had back in town and I'll drill you, Beamis.
Shout and tell her to come out.'

Beamis shook his head. 'Can't do that, Brunton,' he
shouted back. 'Leave her be. She's not involved in this.'

'Like hell,' Brunton shouted. 'She was Chung Wah's
before you got her. She's bound to know where the

double-dealing snake's hiding out. You bring her to me, and you and your buddy can go free. If I have to come down for her, you two are dead men, I promise.'

'Tell him to go shit in his hat, and we'll make a break for it,' Al whispered out of the corner of his mouth. 'Once we're in the canyon we can hold them off till they get old and tired.'

'You got ten seconds before I start shooting,' Brunton shouted. He began to shout the count.

In the split second before Johnny and Al began to make their run for cover the girl stood, and slowly, confidently, she walked out into the open, palms held outward at her side to show she came unarmed.

'No, don't . . .' Beamis shouted, then realized that he did not know her name to call to her, never had time to ask.

'That's good,' came Brunton's harsh voice from the heights above. 'Now, you join her, Beamis, and come a little walk up here where we can parley. Don't try nothing.'

Johnny began walking, hands still raised. When he reached the girl she looked up at him, gave a tight little smile. She really could not let him die for her. Chung Wah had always said Beamis was the best gambler he had ever played against, that he could tell the odds faster than any man. He must have known that he was dead if she did not surrender herself to Brunton, yet he had still refused to trade his life for hers. This *gweh loh* was something else. She gave him another smile, then faced front, began walking alongside him. She could not bear to think what Brunton and his men would do to her. Instead she began praying silently to Kuan Yin, goddess of mercy.

'You didn't have to do this,' Johnny said. 'Al and me had a plan . . .'

'Too late,' she replied, but her voice shook, betraying her fear. 'Thank you for everything you do. But none of this your doing, your fault. Chung Wah do this, I bring you in further. Now I go put it right. You hand me over to Brunton, please, then he let you and your friend go.'

Beamis was silent. There was no time to argue. His brain was in a ferment, trying to think ahead of Brunton, trying to concoct a plan. 'I don't know your name,' he said. ' I thought. . . .'

He couldn't say any more. They both knew why he asked now.

'My name Pah Lee,' she said softly, looking directly at him, her face serious. Oh, if only there had been another time, another place, she thought. Here was a man who would always stand by her. To death, even.

'Polly,' Johnny said, 'That's one hell of a sweet name.'

She thought to correct him, then thought, what the hell, the people who sold her into slavery, her own parents, gave her her name, her own countrymen who could speak the poetry of it, knew what it meant in Chinese, had misused her and abandoned her. Chung Wah, so proud of his separateness and convinced of the superiority of his race, had left her as bait so that he could make his escape. Only an ugly, red-haired foreign devil cared about her, was even prepared to face death for her. Polly sounded good on his lips. Polly she would be.

'Keep walking, you two,' Brunton yelled, as Beamis and Polly reached the sloping trail. 'Come on up here.'

Brunton and his two men stepped out of cover, their rifles levelled on the pair below.

'One thing to remember, Miss Polly,' Johnny said, as they trudged upwards. 'The odds don't look good, maybe, but the game ain't over yet. It's how you play your hand that's important.'

'What I do?' Polly asked.

'Weeel,' Johnny said thoughtfully, 'Brunton thinks one or both of us knows where Chung Wah is hiding out. I guess we play along with that.'

Polly nodded, her brain working overtime. Maybe, just maybe. . . . 'You got an ace in hole, Johnny?' she asked hopefully.

Johnny gave her a surprised look. 'You know what one is?' he asked, smiling in spite of the tight spot they were in.

'Sure,' Polly said, nodding vigorously. 'Chung Wah say all good gamblers have one. He say you one son of a bitch at gambling. You got one, huh?'

He loved her voice, that crazy accent. 'Most decidedly,' he said. 'Just drop back a little, look at my belt.'

She pretended to stumble on the rocky mountain path, stopped momentarily to rub her ankle. Her eyes widened when she saw the Colt stuck in the back of Johnny's pants. A rough shout from above urged her on.

'I got ace in hole too, gambling man,' she said, drawing alongside Johnny Beamis. 'Pretend I not want to go with you. Grab my wrist.'

Johnny did as she said, and felt through the silk of her old dress the hard outline of a slim knife, the one she had recently pressed to Ace Doone's throat.

'I get near enough, I take out that bastard's heart,' she hissed as they trudged upward, nearing Brunton. 'Johnny, when we get close to him, I hang back. You hold me, hand me over to Brunton, please?'

Johnny didn't want to, but when he considered the choices he knew there was no room for passengers.

'OK,' he said unwillingly. 'But be careful, huh? Hate anything to happen to you.' That was as close as he'd ever got to telling a woman she was special to him.

Polly gave him a tight smile. 'You too, *gweh loh*,' she whispered. 'We look out for each other's asses, heh?'

Johnny's eyes whipped round to her. Now, who taught her that one?

'Listen,' she said, looking straight forward at Brunton, who was watching them closely, suspiciously, 'I hang back, start to wail. You grab my arm and drag me, make it look like you sick of me. I play along. Just let me get near him. You go for gun when I stab Brunton, shoot other two.'

'It just might work,' Johnny said, nodding.

Polly sniffed. 'You got better idea, gambling man?'

Johnny grinned. 'No, ma'am.'

Polly gave him a smile, as if to say 'here goes', then sank to her knees on the rocky trail, began to scream and cry, held her hands up to Johnny, who stood transfixed till she hissed to him, 'Grab my arms! Drag me up there! Not like that! Be nasty! You want to live?'

Johnny unwillingly seized Polly's arms and dragged the wailing woman up the trail determinedly, her screams and entreaties echoing off the mountainside.

'Well, well,' Brunton sneered, stepping down the trail to meet the pair, his rifle held steady upon them. 'Ain't so full of sass and grit now, is she, Beamis?'

'Here, take her,' Beamis said, panting and holding his side. The wound was oozing blood once more through his shirt, seeping through the much-washed silk dress of Polly's which was bound tight around Al's crude surgery.

'Seems to me I remember you being pretty definite about not parting with the lady here last time we met,' Brunton said suspiciously. 'What makes you change your mind now?'

Beamis shrugged. 'She ain't worth dying for,' he said begrudgingly.

'You're a small-time loser,' Brunton said, stepping closer, his pop-eyes swivelling between Johnny and Polly. 'Now, where's that rat Chung Wah?'

'She'll take you to him,' Johnny said, and shoved her roughly towards Brunton, whilst watching the two other guys out the corner of his eyes. That was good, they were coming closer now, both on Brunton's left, grinning broadly, thinking they had Beamis and Polly cold. So relaxed in the face of a wounded, unarmed man and a slip of a woman that they were nursing their rifles in the crooks of their arms, the barrels pointing to the floor.

Polly threw herself back on Johnny's chest and began to wail, 'Please, no makee me go with this killer. I take you to Chung Wah. He no go away. I show you where he hide money, gold. You takee, not give me to Blunton. . . .'

'So you do know where the cheating scum's holed up,' Brunton crowed, and he snatched at the girl, grasping her by her left arm. 'Come here, you bitch, you gonna . . .'

Soon as she felt Brunton grip her, Polly released Johnny, and, as fluid as a dancer, she half-turned and fell into Brunton's arms like a lover embracing him. And as she came into his arms her right hand struck upward, and the thin-bladed skinning knife slipped so easily between his ribs, up to the hilt. Rawlins and Deyton suddenly came to life. Realizing that their meal-ticket was in dire trouble they yelled and began to bring their rifles to bear on Polly.

Beamis jumped forward and pushing Polly bodily to the floor yanked at the hoglegged handle of the Colt in the back of his belt. It came smooth and clear into his right hand, and he squeezed the trigger, caught Rawlins full in the chest, and as he pitched, dying to the floor,

Johnny swivelled his pistol through thirty degrees and shot Deyton in the gut as he fired his rifle into the space where Polly had been standing. The bullet whistled harmlessly over her head, narrowly missing Brunton, who was staggering drunkenly on the trail, one hand wrapped around the hilt of the knife stuck up into his chest, the other grappling with the butt of his Peacemaker, trying to pull it from its holster, but it was suddenly heavy and would not come free. The pain in his side was hellish, and he was having trouble focusing his eyes too. As if in a dream he watched Polly rise from the floor and approach him. God, but he wanted to kill her so badly!

'No,' said Polly, as if reading his thoughts. 'You not hurt anyone again.' And she placed one small palm flat in his chest and pushed him backward off the trail on to the treacherous scree slope of the mountainside.

Brunton staggered backwards, digging his heels in, his mouth working soundlessly in an appeal that would not have been heeded anyway, for the last of his followers were dead already. His boots shifted on the scree, the shale beneath him began to slip and slide, and soon the whole mountainside seemed to be moving in a dusty, roaring avalanche. For a moment Brunton seemed to be riding the crest of a huge, stone wave, then he slipped, and the red, sandy surf took him. He was borne down, waist deep, till he hit a rock, and the avalanche surged around him, crushing him. He screamed once out loud, a truly awful scream as of a soul in torment that reached the couple on the trail, causing Beamis to bite his lip and look away and Polly to turn and bury her face in Johnny's chest. Brunton was borne on again. The crest of the wave boiled up around his shoulders, then dragged him under, and he was seen and heard no more.

'Hey, steady now,' said Beamis, resisting the urge to hug Polly back, 'it's all over. We're safe now.' Then as Polly hugged harder, he thought, what the hell, and hugged her back. And it sure felt good.

'You break open my wound again, I'm gonna dig out that scroll and sell you,' Johnny warned her.

Polly laughed shakily and nodded down towards the swamp's edge where Al was standing waiting for them, trying to staunch the wound in his shoulder with a piece torn from his shirt lap.

'Have to use my last dress on him now,' she said.

'Shame,' Johnny said, 'and you had to leave all those beautiful dresses of yours at the Gam Saan, to burn.'

'Those dresses too small,' Polly said. 'They not mine.'

'Then whose . . .' Johnny asked, then leaned back from their embrace and gazed open-mouthed at Polly. She laughed out loud at the expression on his face as it sank in just whose dresses they were.

'I told you he liked to dress up,' she said.

'Ol' Chung Wah was a candypants? A fancy Dan? No kidding?' Beamis asked, shaking his head incredulously. 'You mean. . . ? You and him. . . ? You weren't. . . .?'

Polly laughed ruefully. 'No,' she said. 'I present from Uncle, but Chung Wah not want. What you think of that, Johnny?'

'Not a lot,' said Johnny, pausing to look at her, 'but I sure want you, Miss Polly.'

'Don't worry,' said Polly, still holding on to his hand. 'You got, *gweh loh*!'